Trap Jam

Trap Jam

Steven Barwin

James Lorimer & Company Ltd., Publishers
Toronto

James Lorimer & Company Ltd., Publishers acknowledges the support of the Ontario Arts Council. We acknowledge the support of the Canada Council for the Arts which last year invested $24.3 million in writing and publishing throughout Canada. We acknowledge the Government of Ontario through the Ontario Media Development Corporation's Ontario Book Initiative.

Cover design: Tyler Cleroux
Cover image: Shutterstock

Library and Archives Canada Cataloguing in Publication

Barwin, Steven, author
    Trap jam / Steven Barwin.

(SideStreets)
Issued in print and electronic formats.
ISBN 978-1-4594-1100-5 (paperback).--ISBN 978-1-4594-1101-2 (epub)

    I. Title. II. Series: SideStreets

PS8553.A7836T73 2016   jC813'.54   C2015-907201-8
                                                 C2015-907202-6

| James Lorimer & Company Ltd., Publishers 317 Adelaide Street West, Suite 1002 Toronto, ON, Canada M5V 1P9 www.lorimer.ca | Canadian edition (978-1-4594-1100-5) distributed by: Formac Lorimer Books 5502 Atlantic Street Halifax, NS, Canada B3H 1G4 | American edition (978-1-4594-1103-6) distributed by: Lerner Publishing Group 1251 Washington Ave N Minneapolis, MN, USA 55401 |

Manufactured by Friesens Corporation in Altona, Manitoba, Canada in January 2016.
Job #220108

In memory of my dad,
who showed me that anything is possible.

Chapter 1

Audition

The only thing with a beat was the second hand moving on the clock above the door. Each movement got me closer to the end of the day. My foot started to tap in time. My pencil gently added in the rhythm, basic quarter note plus triple time, against the ring of my binder. All three sounds meshed together and formed the beat.

I started to rap in my head.

Time's always stuck like it's forever,
when them hands gonna move, never,
forever.
All I want to do is run outta here,
it's just the same old game, come on
already, cut to the next frame.
Rotting in this jail cell I'm a wreck,
hit the deck, this must be a ship-
wreck.

A text vibrated in my pocket. It was the location and time I'd been waiting for:

4:15. Tom's. Just bring your sticks.

When the bell rang, I moved with excitement through the hallways, grabbing my stuff from my locker. Just like that, I was quickly through the doors. I rushed, speedwalking to get out on the street before it was filled with other Harbord Collegiate students scrambling for freedom.

3:50. I had just enough time to make a quick stop at a coffee shop washroom. I wanted to look the part. I changed into my favourite outfit: purple jeans and an off-the-shoulder black studded top. I applied black eyeliner and checked my hair in the mirror. I noticed my hand was shaking, and for a brief second, I thought about backing out. I put my black and red headphones on and turned up the music to block out the toxic thoughts. I marched out onto the street. Music pumped into me, like confidence pouring in. I couldn't stop from rapping softly.

It's now or never, girl when are you going to ever?
Time to get psyched up, because it's you who's sup.
You the real thing, the real deal, you the girl with the ca-ching.

I took a big breath in front of Tom's.

Pulling my headphones down around my neck, I entered. The front part of the store was not busy with people, but it was crammed with instruments filling every inch of wall and floor space. I found the drum section in the second room. The sets were awesome. Most way out of my league. There were some Evolution drum kits and some classic Yamahas. It was like being in a candy store. I wanted it all.

A man with a bushy beard approached me. "Can I help you with anything?"

I eyed the name Carl on his brown music store vest.

"I'm looking for Eddie. Is he around?"

"Yep, I'll grab him for you."

I scanned the drum area again and Eddie appeared, wearing dark jeans, a V-neck T-shirt and a matching employee vest. "Olivia?"

"Yes. I'm here for the audition."

"Thank you for coming in. We're just waiting for . . . oh, there he is. Lucas, this is Olivia."

I see him round the corner, hands in his pockets and white headphones dangling around the collar of his blue shirt. This Lucas guy had the look. He smiled and said, "Hello," in a raspy voice. "How long you been here?"

"She just got here. Should we start?"

"Yeah," I nodded. "Where we doing this?"

Eddie pointed to a nearby drum kit. He extended his hands. "Hop on."

I pulled my sticks from my backpack and sat on the drum stool, getting comfortable. "Is there anything you'd like me to play?"

"What do you think, Lucas?"

"Nah, play whatever you think rocks."

I looked around. There were a few customers milling around.

"Don't worry about them," Eddie said. "People come in and bang on the skins and rip away at the guitars all the time."

I tapped my sticks together, counting out, "One, two, three and four," while stepping heavily onto the bass drum at the same time.

Then I let my sticks loose. Like a wave, the music took control of my limbs. I was at its mercy. I banged my sticks directly onto the snares. Then to impress the guys, I performed some crossovers, changing the tempo each time. I switched to some hi-hat variations to get that grooving metal sound. To even out the sound, I jammed in a base, snare and hi-hat combo.

Suddenly, Lucas held out his hands. "Stop, stop."

I rested my drumsticks on the snare drum. "I'm sorry. What's wrong?"

"What was that?"

"Come on, Lucas," Eddie started, "don't be like that."

"It was an original I've been working on. But I know it's probably not that great. Let me play you something else. Please."

"No. Not at all. It was great," said Lucas. "I mean, I looked at you and I totally didn't expect that. Not that there's anything wrong with you. Um, okay, now this is all coming out wrong."

I stared at Lucas and wondered what he was really thinking. Did he hate it?

"I think what he's saying," Eddie said, "is that you're really good."

"Yeah, you are." Lucas crouched down to look me in the eye where I was sitting. "I can totally attach some vocals on that. Turn it into a song."

"So you're the lead singer?"

"Yeah. And I also play guitar." He stood and placed his hands on Eddie's shoulder. "This guy, he's one of the best DJ scratchers out there. Total natural spinner."

"What can I say, DJ Ed loves to spin the vinyl."

"He also likes to refer to himself in the third person." Lucas laughed. "And he plays some mean keys."

"I like the name."

"Well thank you, Olivia. I think DJ

Ed — it's like I am *educating* people on my music."

Lucas looks at Eddie. "Nicely done. I like her already."

I covered my embarrassment with a smile. *Was this what fitting in a band felt like? Did I make the band?* "So is this a new band or would I be replacing someone? I meant, if I got it."

"Eddie's been our drummer."

"What Lucas means is that I've been running a drum machine. But we want to branch out. A real drummer adds a whole different texture to our sound."

This was a great opportunity. I just hoped they didn't see me as the kid I am. *If they asked me how old I am, do I tell them I'm sixteen? Or do I lie?*

Chapter 2

Interview

Playing in a band with real gigs would be a huge step up. Our high school band is good. I even joined the samba band this year, performing at a few festivals. But I wanted to play *my* music.

"So thank you for letting me try out for your band," I said.

"Hold on," Lucas said. "We aren't done. First I want to hear more, but don't you have any questions for us? I know I've got a bunch for you."

"How long you been playing music?" I asked.

"I'll go first," Lucas jumped in. "Ever since I wanted to be popular, rich and go somewhere in life."

I smiled. Interesting answer.

We were interrupted when a man stopped by wondering if everything is okay.

Eddie introduced the man as his boss. He asked how I liked the drum set.

I thought fast. "It's got a really full sound, but I'm a little worried about some of the reviews it got online."

Eddie did a bad job of hiding a smirk as his boss blabbed on about the importance of personal feel over public reviews. A customer stepped in to ask Eddie some questions about the bongos, and I stepped away from the drums and told the manager I would think about it.

I exited the store and stopped on the sidewalk. After standing out front for a minute or so, feeling stupid, I turned to walk away. *Maybe I will go back to the coffee shop and get a latte.*

A voice behind me said, "That was hilarious!"

It was Eddie, followed by Lucas. "Are you still interested in joining the band?"

"Yes!"

"Well, let's finish the interview, then."

"I'm not on break for another hour," Eddie said.

"Don't worry, I'll take it from here." Lucas pointed. "There's a great pub across the street." I looked and saw one of the places where the university students hang out.

The only time I've been in a pub was for brunch. *Do I need ID?* I stopped.

"Everything okay?"

"I just realized I don't have my wallet on me."

"Oh that's okay. I'll spot you."

The pub had paisley carpet and deep red leather booths. Fans spun from the ceiling and we were seated at a table for two.

"What'll you have?" Lucas asked while the waitress waited.

"Diet Coke."

"No, this is an interview for a band. Have a proper drink."

"Okay . . . I'll have a Coke."

Lucas laughed. He turned to the waitress. "Beer for me, please. Whatever you have on tap."

"I'll need to see some ID," the waitress asked.

Lucas opened his wallet and handed it to her. After some examination, she returned it.

We sat quietly until the drinks appeared before us.

Lucas took a sip. "You're kind of shy. I mean when you're not behind the drums."

I hid behind my Coke.

"Where did you first start to play drums?" he continued.

"I couldn't sit still in school. I was constantly tapping my fingers . . . then my foot and pencil.

Playing the drums always calmed that."

I sipped my drink, trying to think of questions to ask him.

"You ever play in a band before?" Lucas asked.

"High school. Pretty boring, though."

"We all have to start somewhere. So you're at the University of Toronto?"

"Yep." The lie came out too quickly, unfiltered.

"Eddie and me, too. What's your major?"

I took another sip to think. "Thinking about math, but I'm only in my first year. What about you?"

"I'm majoring in getting the hell out of my crappy life and making it big. University is not really my thing. Just putting in the time. Mostly I do bird courses like sociology."

I laughed with a hint of nervousness.

He downed the rest of his beer. "So does Eddie have your number?"

"Yes."

"Mind giving it to me? I make most of the decisions for us."

He held out his phone and I typed in my number.

"Cool. Can I take a photo of you?"

"Ahh . . . sure. Why?"

"We're looking at lots of people. A face tells me a lot more than a name."

I nodded and posed as he took several photos. Then he got up and put cash on the table. "What's the mix?"

"My dad's Cuban and my mom's Jamaican."

"Nice," he said, looking me up and down with a smile. "Let me talk to Eddie, and I'll call in a few days."

"Thanks for the audition. It was really nice to meet you."

He gave me a nod and left.

I sat alone. Just an underage girl in a bar in the middle of the day with a cute university guy. A little giddy, I took a few more sips and took off for home.

Chapter 3

Destiny

When I got my fake ID, I smiled at the made-up name and address on the card — Olivia Kate Smith from Gravenhurst, Ontario. Born four years before me. The face on the card was mine, but that's it.

I got stupid excited the first time I was able to order a beer. The waitress stared at the card and at me, trying to figure it out.

For three months, since making the band, I've been rushing out after school to a dingy shed behind a fraternity house near the University of Toronto campus for rehearsals. The space barely fit us, but I couldn't complain because I wasn't the one paying for it. If we weren't rehearsing, then I was in my room practising. I had to tell my dad I joined a band. It was way obvious. He'd ask questions and I'd tell him a little about Lucas and Eddie, how they were nice boys from the Catholic high school.

I made sure to be on time for dinner with my dad because of Tuesday nights. What Dad thought were "group project nights" were performances at BoomBoom.

The band took on the name Maximum Gray even though the boys weren't completely settled on it. Me, I was just thrilled to be playing live music.

"And for our last song," I said with my mouth pressed against the mic, "here's our cover version of 'OMG' by Usher." I held up my sticks, clapping them together. Lucas ran his fingers through his black hair, wavy and flowing on top, shaved around the sides. He started the intro of the song with his raspy, smooth, perfectly pitched voice. The stage lights kicked into hyperdrive, moving in every direction.

We were just an opening act, the crowd warmer. But Tuesday had quickly become my favourite night of the week. There were only a few dancers on the floor and a small audience sipping drinks at tables, but I was transported whenever we played.

When Lucas's intro heated up, he turned to me with a grin. For just a moment, we locked eyes. That was my cue to jump in.

My right foot pushed down on the bass drum's pedal with aggression. Eddie pounded on his electric keyboard; it shook with every push on the keys.

Lucas and Eddie played off each other. Tonight Lucas was unshaven, looking tough and rugged in ripped jeans and a white shirt that clung nicely to his body. Eddie was still rockin' the goatee and had on black pants, a baseball cap and a checkered shirt.

I threw in some vocals — "oh, oh, oh, oh, oh" — pressing more firmly against the skins with each one. Lucas looked back at me again, throwing a smile between words. It was another cue to back off the drumbeats for his solo. Eddie laid off the keyboards and we both grooved to Lucas as he went big with his vocals. He pulled the song to a close, and I slid my sticks into their black leather holder and stepped off the stage.

"Kickin' performance." Lucas held out a high-five for Eddie and then me. "I'll get us a table."

I visited the washroom to wipe away some sweat and send a text to my dad that study group was running late. His little girl hard at work on her project. When I stepped out, Lucas and Eddie waved me over. "Give me a sec," I told them, then I found an opening at the bar and waited for Raymond.

He noticed me. My new friend wore a tattered apron and was busy placing dirty plates and glasses into a dishwashing bucket. "Great performance, Olivia. Beats were harsh," Raymond said, rolling his *R*s.

"Thank you," I said as I did a short bow. "Any news?"

He shook his head. "I check every day, hoping."

"Well, George Brown College doesn't know what it's missing. I know you're going to get it eventually."

"Can't thank you enough for helping with the application . . . for everything."

"And I can't thank *you* enough for the fake ID. George Brown would be stupid not to accept you. You're going to be a fantastic chef."

Lucas called me.

"Gotta go." I crossed my fingers. "Maybe tomorrow."

At the table Lucas asked, "Why you always talking to that guy?"

"I'm helping him apply for a scholarship to get into college."

"But he's a dishwasher. You going to clean dishes for him?"

"He's trying to get into college."

"In Mexico?"

"No. Here!"

"I think it's a noble thing you're doing, Olivia," said Eddie. "I'm racking up a hefty student loan. Wish you'd been around to help me apply for a scholarship when I started."

Lucas wore a big smirk. "Thanks for the sappy life story."

"Thank you, Eddie." I turned to Lucas. "And, Raymond is from Quito, Ecuador. Not Mexico."

I took a sip of my drink. The one problem with playing at a club was that drinks were discounted for band members. Well, I guess that wasn't really a problem.

After a long sip, Lucas said, "Now that this is working, we need to take our band to the next level. I want to play bigger venues."

I nodded. "Yeah, but we also have to build our way up. And I think it comes from finding ourselves, musically."

Eddie said, "She's right, you know. Just looking at the jam session after the third song."

"Yeah," I said excitedly, "the beat was just pouring out of me. And your rapping — "

"Same thing. I was just letting go. Giving in to your beat," Eddie added

Lucas put his beer glass down. "I'm not saying that wasn't great, but it was kind of crap. There was no connection to the song I was singing."

"That's the point," Eddie said. "I'd love to record that stuff."

I said, "That's a great idea!" almost spilling my beer.

"Yeah, but guys, we have to stick with the

program. My band needs to be on the same page."

Eddie and I looked at each other and the same time said, "Your band?"

"Ours, mine, yours — it's all the same thing. Here's my point. Just think about the artists you look up to. They keep thinking bigger and better."

"Well, 'better' I agree with," Eddie said, "but we also have to study. You need to give it time."

"Yeah, homework is intense." Referring to my fake university studies had become automatic for me.

"You have to decide if you're a student or a musician," said Lucas. "In this business, if you wait too long, you become ancient."

As the new member, I let them fight it out. Another round of drinks came to the rescue. Then Lucas asked, "So how are we going to the next level? Think about it, and I'll be right back."

Lucas left, and Eddie and I turned to each

other. Eddie said in a lowered tone, "He didn't like what we did because he wasn't singing."

"He felt left out," I said, a little tired of making the same excuses for Lucas all the time.

"Sometimes I think he *should* be left out. There are better singers out there."

I didn't respond. Was all the band politics the price I had to pay for just playing music?

Eddie moved the glasses of beer to one side and edged closer to the table. "I'm a hip-hop guy. That's my thing and I'm used to using drum machines. Set the beat and leave it. But with you playing and us reading off each other . . . our sound is pretty unique. What do you think?"

"I agree. Your rhythm and your rap, I just find it easy to drum off of."

"There's something called trap music. Ever heard of it?"

"No."

"It's all about intensive rap with kickin' drums. What we were doing was kind of like a live trap sound. Except, real trap music has got a sound that's so uptempo. Our sound is deeper, more complex. With some serious baseline drumming, rap vocals mixed in . . . It's the kind of unique sound that could get us noticed."

"Only problem is convincing Lucas," I said.

"He just wants a danceable chorus to showcase his voice." He checked over his shoulder. "Lucas will be back any minute. I have a quick question for you."

"Yeah, go ahead."

"Are you lying about your age? You're not really nineteen, are you?"

I was shocked. How did he know? Was it something I said? Had I slipped up in my story as the other Olivia?

Lucas returned, placing his hand on my shoulder. I realized that he needed help standing up. "So, what do you guys have for me?"

We all looked at each other.

Still stunned by Eddie's question, I took a sip from my beer. It was empty, no matter how high I tipped the glass.

"I'll bite," Eddie said. "I vote for a newer sound for our band plus a better website. Something more professional with samples of our music, maybe a few vids."

I took the middle ground, wanting to try more new material but also have more rehearsal time. As much as I wanted to explore the trap sound Eddie talked about, I couldn't be the one to tell that to Lucas.

Lucas looked sceptical. "Just remember who started this band. And I can end it, too."

The one thing we could all agree on was getting food.

Chapter 4

Night Bird

Equipment packed, we hit a cheap Chinese restaurant. The place was crowded with university students. It was a bit grimy and musty, but at least it was cheap.

"Don't know much about this Chinese general," Lucas said loud enough for every table in the restaurant to hear, "but I love his chicken, man!"

We cheered with Chinese beer.

Eddie read off the phone in his hand, "This

dish is named after General Tso Tsung-tang from the Qing dynasty."

We all laughed. I don't exactly know why, but after a few drinks, everything was funnier. The manager's eyes found us, so I focused on eating. I was so hungry, I almost drank the sweet and sour sauce from its saucer. The boys demanded more beers and free refills of steamed rice. A quick scan of my phone showed a quarter to eleven. My dad would kill me if he knew where I was . . . and that I was probably a bit drunk. I threw him a quick text just to let him know that I was running late with the study group and that I'd be home soon. He'd be happy that I was mature enough to keep him updated.

"Rice is like bread at an Italian restaurant," Lucas insisted to the waitress. "You don't charge for it."

The waitress smiled with her pen perched above her small pad.

"Just let it go," I said.

I guess the restaurant had had enough because the manager finally stepped in, sending our waitress away. With a not-so-pleased glare, he placed the bill on our table. He insisted that we pay and leave.

Lucas wasn't scared of him. Seriously, I'd never seen Lucas scared of anyone.

"Not until we get our fortune cookies, " Lucas answered, half-drunk, with a mouthful of food.

"Boys, let's just go." The manager rolled his eyes and I knew our time was up. He wanted us to pay first, but Lucas stayed determined.

I grabbed one of the beers and downed what was left while I could. I took out all I had — ten bucks — and put in Lucas's hand. "Just pay him."

The manager snapped his fingers and fortune cookies appeared on the table.

Cookies and guitar case in hand, Lucas led us out. We loitered around the front while Lucas and Eddie made impressions of the headless chickens and pigs hanging in the front display.

We whispered loudly as we got on the late-night streetcar. The boys laughed at me as I tried to walk to my seat while the car was moving, my legs all wobbly. Seated, we cracked open our cookies.

"Check this out," Eddie said. "'Wise are they who do not believe they are wise.'"

Lucas said, "Eddie's using that one on his next essay," and we all laughed. "Mine says, 'If you continue to give, you'll continue to have.'"

"Then why do I continue to want?" Eddie said and we laughed again.

"Could be our next big hit," I said, "the fortune cookie song." I pressed my feet against the seat in front of me and read mine. "'The most obvious solution is not always the best.'" I looked at the boys. "So deep."

Eddie was on his phone again. "Already a fortune cookie song."

"You know," I said, "that thing doesn't have all the answers."

He smiled. "With Google and YouTube on my side, I'll have to disagree. This is my stop." He disappeared down the stairs and onto the street.

Lucas scrunched closer to me. Our working partnership had morphed into something more. We just seemed to mesh so I decided to explore it. Lucas was more mature than all the high school boys I knew combined.

Each jerk of the streetcar felt like a wild ride. I closed my eyes, attempting to push back the feeling of throwing up. "Too much . . ." I rested my head on his shoulder.

"No such thing. These are our college years. We're supposed to overindulge."

At the university stop, I was grateful to breathe in some fresh air.

"That was a fun night. Plus we made a little money," Lucas said as we got off the streetcar.

"Yeah," I said with as much enthusiasm as

I could muster. We were only at the university bookstore. The thought of the long walk home was starting to concern me.

Lucas said, "You should write a song about it. Something to accompany the fortune cookie ditty."

"The beer song," I suggested. He laughed, so I started singing, just off the top of my head, throwing in a country twang for fun. "My boyfriend poured me a tall one, my favourite of all the ales. And then he poured four more —"

Lucas jumped in. "And I kept drinking them back, must've been at least two pails."

We looked at each other and I finished big with, "Of my favourite ales!"

Lucas pulled me close and kissed me. I tried not to break it with a smile.

"Lucas?"

"Olivia. This feels right."

We kissed some more.

He pulled back and asked, softly, "Come up to my place?"

I looked up at the dorm building. "You said you have a test."

"I like what we have. The band, the friendship . . ."

"What about Eddie?" I asked.

"Don't worry about him." He put his hand on face. "You're in my band, but I hardly know anything about you. I want to know more."

I felt protected in his arms. "So, what you're saying is that this girl Olivia is an enigma."

Lucas nodded, smiling. "Yes, this woman is a mystery."

I was surrounded by Lucas's warmth and it felt good. His hand on my arm sent a spark through my body. "Intrigued?" I asked.

That got another kiss, a longer, gentler, sweeter kiss.

"I don't want to be one of those guys who pressures girls. So, if you don't want to, you don't have to come up." He reached into his pocket, took out a square package and locked it in my hand. "You're in control. Your call, Olivia."

Lucas entered the dorm, and I turned and walked away. I unclenched my hand and looked down. I didn't know what to expect, maybe a key to his room or maybe a metal guitar clip for my necklace. I did not expect a condom.

I continued up St. George Street past the big library building. I had never held a condom in my hand so I slowly ripped it open. Inside was a squishy rubber tube. I touched the condom, squealed and shoved it back in the wrapper before tossing it into a garbage can.

Turning onto Bloor Street I passed restaurants with large blue and green overflowing bins in front. I turned up the next one-way street and stopped in front of a brown two-storey house. I slowly unlocked the front door, crept up the stairs and saw my dad's bedroom light turn off. I slid quietly into my room, heart still racing as I thought of Lucas.

Chapter 5

Crash

I was hungover. My head throbbed. As I slouched down the hall, my algebra teacher, Mr. Wallace, ordered me to take off my sunglasses and put down my hood. I did, wanting to avoid the office and trouble. The buzzing bright fluorescent lights were killing me. I ducked into the washroom and was able to hide for a bit in an empty stall before class started.

Later, I sat with my head on my binder and waited for the blaring announcements to end. Ms. Cooper, the science teacher, finished off attendance and said, "This is a reminder that your fluids test is next class. Today is review day." I looked at the people on either side of me. This was news to me, but clearly not to them. The only thing in my binder was a map of the University of Toronto and a sample first-year schedule I grabbed online.

Ms. Cooper went on. "Think about pouring water and glue into two separate beakers. Which will fill up faster and why?"

Next to me, the hand of the girl in a cream baby-doll dress and long necklace shot up. "Water, because glue has greater viscosity. It is thicker."

"That's right. The glue has a greater resistance to flow."

I leaned toward the girl with my phone. "Can I snap a few photos of your notes?"

She just looked at me.

"What? I've been away. I had surgery," I added.

Still no response. She didn't buy my lie. Not even a "How you feeling?" Maybe she was put off by the purple tint I put in my hair yesterday while I was "sick." Or maybe it was the kicking red boots I bought last week. "Never mind," I said.

I slid the phone under my notebook, which was pretty sparse except for some doodles and random lyrics to a song I was brainstorming for the band. Ms. Cooper asked another question and the girl in the baby-doll dress jumped at it, squawking a big response. I did a fake stretch and snapped some quick shots of her work. Well, what she doesn't know can only help me.

The second half of the class was a lab. I slunk in my chair hoping to be ignored, not knowing which group I was in, not wanting to be in any.

Then Ms. Know-It-All sidled up beside me and I was a little annoyed. What could she want now? But then she said, "You forgot?

Lab partners?" She pointed to a posted list of groups before returning to her set of beakers.

I responded, "We are," without much conviction. Not my fault. I have more important things that demand my attention. Maximum Gray.

I stood next to her as she read the temperature of a small jar of ketchup and checked something off a worksheet.

"It was just day surgery."

She didn't even look up at me. Just at the ketchup.

I looked down at her binder and took note of the name: Elizabeth. Lizzy. I knew that.

She caught me looking and said, "Not a chance. Get your own notes. We may be partners but that's it."

"What you don't know, Lizzy, is that you get what you give. I play in a band and could've gotten you into club BoomBoom or Jive for free. Maybe even a nice drink."

"You have to be nineteen to get into those

clubs and to drink. Oh, were you held back?"

"Well, following every single rule gets you nowhere in life."

"So, hold on. You're admitting that you drink?"

I eyed another corner of her juicy notes sticking out of that binder. I picked up the second jar and spilt a little of whatever was in it.

"Hey, that's honey!"

She ran to get paper towel. I got my pictures and spent the rest of the period watching her do the experiment.

The bell sounded like a siren going off in my head. On the way to the next class, I started to thumb through the photos on my phone. They were either horribly blurry or cut off by an elbow. I tried to pinch-in on the screen, but then they looked more like pieces of abstract art than science notes.

This sucked. My dad would flip out if I failed another test. His warning was clear. One more and it's meeting time. Ms. Cooper plus the principal equalled hell for me.

Out in the hall, Cal, jock extraordinaire, jostled me as he pushed past. A rescue light lit up in the bottom of my brain. You had to carry at least a B average to stay on a school team. He might just be my saving grace. I batted the lashes over my red eyes. "Cal."

"Hey, Olivia. What's up?" he answered, which was funny, because he towered over everyone. I sidled beside him and walked with him down the hallway.

"Playing drums in a band. Counting the days till high school's over."

"You mean, counting the years."

I laughed, trying to not make it sound fake. I playfully touched his arm and went in for the kill. "So how're things on the football team?"

"It's basketball. Are you okay?"

"Me?" *Don't say hungover,* I told myself over and over again. "Just a bit of a headache. Did you hear about my surgery?"

"No. But I've been at tournaments."

"So, basketball?" I stammered.

"It's going well. Pretty excited for the area tournament that's coming up. So, do you guys do gigs?"

"Yeah, all the time."

"Where?"

Reveal nothing, I told myself. Skirt the incriminating truth. "Wherever they will have us. Coffee shops, old-age homes. So, I'm short on science notes for the test. Can you help me out?" I asked.

"Of course." He stopped with a look of surprise on his face. "No one's ever asked me for notes before."

"Come on — really? You're a smart guy. Plus, don't you have to maintain a B to play on the team?"

"Yeah, more like a B minus."

I pulled out my phone while he unzipped his binder.

"There you go. All yours."

I stood there, my finger frozen on the camera button. The notes were sketchy, point form at best. He also liked to draw stickmen shooting basketballs into nets and doodle cat faces.

"Sorry. It's kind of messy."

I couldn't drum up the words to offer even a small compliment. I wondered if he realized that I hadn't taken a picture yet. I reminded myself of my newest mantra: Beggars can't be choosers. "No. Jeez. Cal. Thank you," I mumbled. I was really scraping the bottom of the barrel. Those were probably the lowest, stuck to the bottom of the barrel B minus notes. But with a few clicks, at least *some* science notes were securely on my phone and I could relax through Family Studies.

Chapter 6

Secrets

My dad and I were somewhere between Funk and Jazz on our way to Rhythm and Blues in the used record store. I picked up an album and examined its cover. Eddie had a huge collection of records that looked just like these in his apartment.

I looked over the top of the album when my dad said, "How's my girl doing?"

I shrugged, my mind still on a romantic text that Lucas sent earlier.

My eyes want to see you, my lips want to kiss you.

"She seems somewhere else, far away. I want to know why she's stressed out. Why she's not enjoying some of the best memory-making years of her life. Does she have friends at school? A crush on a boy? I love her passion for music, but what about a sport?"

I put the record album down. His questions made me feel bad. I knew he was worried about me but not this much. I loved him and I did hate lying to him. It was extra-hard when I was sober.

I just needed to be me, to find me. My music was taking me places, opening doors I never thought possible. But there was no way Dad would understand that or let me continue if he knew that the other guys in the band were in university. I had shown up at some used music equipment store, banged a few riffs and beats on the drums, and next thing I knew, I was in.

I caught him looking at my phone. The

smart move was to give my dad something. "I have a crush. It's Lucas."

My dad nodded. "The boy in the band with you. Does he know you like him?"

"Yes."

"Is he the source of all those mystery texts that make you smile?"

I nodded, a little embarrassed that he picked up on that.

"What about the ones that make you light up like a rock and roll light show?"

"Those would be about the band. About the music."

"Thank you for your honesty. Mind if I ask you another question?"

"Okay."

"Are you okay?"

A laugh escaped, but I wasn't sure why. "Yes."

He seemed relieved. "It might not seem like it sometimes, but I'm always here for you."

A voice broke into our father–daughter moment. "Hey, it's you."

He was standing in front of the Punk Rock section in the next aisle. He had a university logo on his backpack and a full-on ducktail beard. And he was walking toward me.

"I saw you at that club, the Ruby . . ."

And just like that, *poof*, my new life was about to go up in smoke.

Before I could come up with a response, my dad looked at him and said, "You've got the wrong person."

But the guy was right. Yep, that was me. It had been a great crowd, decent pay and a hard-to-get gig at the Ruby Star the month before.

"Sorry, but I don't do clubs."

"That's weird, because you look exactly like —"

"Hey, get lost," my dad said as he put his arm around me and guided me away.

The guy offered my dad an apology, but it didn't matter because we were on our way out the door.

Disaster averted.

* * *

At home and tucked away in my bedroom, I stared at my textbook. I had to push my song notebook to the side. I couldn't help it if studying for a science test made me think of song lyrics. All I had was:

Can't focus. Buzzin in my mind.
Not enough study notes. Bogus waste of time.

What does it matter? I thought. *I'll never use this stuff anyway.*

The longer I stared at the science textbook, the less it made sense. The information on viscosity could have been in a foreign language: "A Newtonian is a material whose viscosity value is the same at all shear rates." What's a shear rate and why should I care?

Desperate for a shortcut, I picked up my phone and found Cal's notes. Again, no matter how much I zoomed in, I couldn't decipher the blurry words. So much for my B minus.

My dad knocked on the door and slowly opened it. He seemed surprised and pleased that I was buried in homework. "Doing okay?"

I nodded.

"Need help?"

I sighed. "Thanks, but not now."

He turned and closed the door.

The house has been quiet ever since Mom left. Dad doesn't say bad stuff about her. Maybe he still loves her. Or maybe he doesn't want me to feel bad about looking like her. "You have her eyes," my grandmother used to tell me. It sounded like a curse. "Nose, too," a cousin would add, like they could actually tell.

But before Granny died, I got all the details. My mom got depressed or anxious or both and started smoking joints, even leaving them around. According to Granny, I picked one up when I was two and tried to eat it. My first buzz. By the time I was in preschool, it was harder stuff. Seems Mom would be too strung out to pick me up. That's if she was home at all.

I don't really remember any of that. But maybe it's why in a club full of chances to do drugs, I choose to drink.

My phone buzzed. It was Lucas.

Thinking about you. Want to go out?

Studying

So?

And in bed

:) Want me to come over?

I smiled. Then felt weird, thinking about what my dad had noticed.

No

After a few moments, my phone rang.

"Hey, Lucas. I can't see you tonight."

"It's just business. We have a gig tomorrow night. I also wanted to talk about our new band's name."

"We have a new name already?"

"No. We need one."

"I'm studying."

"Boring." I could hear him snoring.

"See ya."

"Fine."

I tossed my phone onto my night table and returned to studying. It was hard to focus my science-mumbo-jumbo-soaked brain. Antsy, I got out of bed and crept downstairs, careful of every creak. In the living room, I opened my dad's liquor cabinet and swivelled off the cap of one of the bottles. I took a swill. It burned nicely and had the perfect viscosity as it travelled its way through my body.

Chapter 7

Shooting Star

It took some force to slide open the rusty door of the fraternity house shed. It was stuffed with an assortment of old bike parts, a car tire and a rusted-out washer and dryer. Luckily, there was just enough space — a cleared-out cement-floored section — to hold our equipment and allow for us to practise.

Lucas had helped me get a used drum kit from the store where he worked. My dad had helped with the money. It was really an awesome rockin' set. It was smaller than my set at home but easier for the gigs. The four-piece shell pack, Ludwig Breakbeats by Questlove, has a bass drum, floor tom, tom and wood snare. The bass has a huge booming sound and the toms sing heavenly. Lucas even helped me to tweak a few things like the heads on the snare. Eddie said it was a small kit with a big sound — like me.

I flumped down on the drum's stool. "Sorry I'm late. Bad day."

Lucas asked, "That time of the month?"

"Shut up!" I said a little annoyed and disgusted. "Teacher held me back —"

Eddie asked, "You mean, professor?" from a beat-up beanbag chair.

"Yeah. Same thing." I threw down some drumroll warm-ups, trying to ignore the boys. A while back, Dad had found a drummer to coach me. She believed that playing drums was like running a marathon. Unless you warmed your body, you could pull something and take yourself out of the race. I started to work through some basic rudimental exercises, kind of like scales in piano. I varied speed and dynamics, such as flams, paradiddles, single stroke rolls, stickings and feet exercises.

I made sure I was warming all the areas that would be involved during the gig. I was getting the blood flowing. Once my whole body is working together, I just play open. I get into a good grove, playing whatever I feel in the moment, just for fun. Warming up might sound like a lot of work, but it doesn't take long and then I am really ready to rock.

Lucas stepped closer to me, his guitar slung over his shoulder. "How'd the test go?"

"Intro to Chemistry exam was hard. I hear Mr. Senka likes to scare students and then bell curve up. But it doesn't really matter because I'll make it up during the lab work." I smiled. I was proud that I had memorized my schedule, some first-year course names, professors and teaching assistants, and some of the jargon.

Course ratings on the Internet got me the information, and then I drilled it into my brain like I was practising drumming. If my high school marks were on drumming or details of my fake life, I'd be pulling As.

Lucas stepped toward me and grabbed my hand. The sensation sent an electric jolt up my arm and through my body. "All that matters is that you passed."

I nodded and said, "Lucky for me, it was multiple choice." That, sadly, described my high school chemistry test. With bad study notes and a little hungover, I think I scraped by with a 70 percent.

Eddie coughed loudly. "If you need me, I'll be —"

Lucas released my hand. "No. Let's refocus." He balanced his phone on a box and hit Record. "Time to jam!"

I gripped my sticks between my thumbs and forefingers, ready to lose myself in the music. I closed my eyes and waited for Eddie to find a tempo on electric keyboard, and I jumped in. We'd decided to bring in the keyboard for a few songs to add variety. Lucas threw in some impromptu lyrics, which were mostly grunt sounds with the odd word thrown in. I was still able to groove to it.

It was like walking through the different genres at the used music store. Our musical range went from pop to funk to R&B. Often we switched on the fly. To complement the eighth notes, I counted quietly in the background of my head. One, two, three, four . . . foot on the bass drum on the one and three. Snare on the two and four. I threw in some cymbals because it felt great.

As soon as Eddie and I infused some trap sounds, Lucas started to bail and the music started to get clumsy and fall apart. Lucas stopped recording.

"Come on, man," Eddie said. "I think we have something here."

"I'm not convinced." Lucas brushed his

hand through his hair. "I want to talk to you guys about band names."

"I'd rather continue to jam," I said.

Eddie backed me up. "Totally agree. Maximum Gray is cool. Plus the club knows us as that."

Lucas bulldozed over what we had to say. "Yes, Maximum Gray's a killer name. I just don't know if it's right for how far we've come and where we are as a band right now."

Eddie said, "I always said it sounded good — even if it doesn't make much sense."

The two boys ignored me and an argument broke out over the renaming of our band. They fought a lot. Drama can be fun, but it was often a waste of time we could have spent on the music. After the fireworks, Lucas would always come to me to complain about Eddie and to rehash the moment. What he was really looking for was for me to say that I agreed with him. Truth was that I always sided with Eddie. Lucas accused me of not supporting him every time I wasn't completely enthusiastic for his cause. I'd tell him to let it go, but Lucas held onto things. He was a grudge keeper. But I even found his grudge-keeping hot. What can I say? I was a sucker for someone who felt a passion for music, even if it was just about the name of a band.

Eddie slapped his hands down hard against his thighs. "You know, I've only got a limited amount of time here. I've got a big essay —"

"The band comes first."

"That's easy for you to say. Your parents pay your tuition. I don't do well, I don't get to come back next semester."

Lucas stood. "Am I the only one who wants to make it big? Go platinum?"

"Fine!" Eddie said, "you pick the name. Whatever you want."

"Radioactive Ammo." Lucas's smile was big.

Lucas liked to switch band names as often as he liked to switch cases for his phone.

"Now," Lucas started, "We have to get some PR. What about trying out for a reality music television show —"

Eddie cut him off. "Those are rigged. They string you along but they already know who's going to win. We could play some festivals but they are hard to get in. Plus, no one knows Atomic Ammo —"

Lucas cut in, "Radioactive Ammo."

Tired of not jamming, I said, "Let's focus on writing songs before we go there. Something that comes from our experiences. We need to write about life, love —"

"So . . ." Lucas started, "you want me to write a song about you?"

"That's not the point at all!"

Eddie said, "What she's saying, Lucas, is that —"

"You don't have to tell me what she's saying. I'm not stupid."

I needed to do something before this jam session turned into our last. I slammed my hand down onto my snare drum.

There was silence.

After a long moment, Eddie said, "I saw a poster for this huge soup festival in the Beaches. Chefs from all types of restaurants will be handing out soup to raise money for some charity. Plus, there's going to be a main stage for bands to play."

Really? Soup?

Lucas jumped up. "Let's write a soup song!"

Both guys looked at me like I was a soup expert or a lyrics machine or crazy. Well, it was better than arguing. I started a three-sixteenth note. Slowly I sizzled in the hi-hats, then some lyrics.

Jumbo, gumbo, goulash and gazpacho.

Lucas jived in.

I paused. "More?"

They nodded and I continued the riff.

*Egg-drop, French onion and miso, too.
Don't eat shark fin, it's a big big
taboo.*

Lucas clapped his hands. "Needs some work, but it's good."

"You think?" I said.

"But, I say we open our soup festival set with it."

"Yeah," Eddie said. "Show us as a serious band, but it also lets the audience know that we have a sense of humour."

Lucas nodded. "Plus, as Olivia said, it's good to be different. New beat. Corny lyrics. Playing to the show. It might be bad press but it would be press."

"Better yet," I said, half-joking, "we can get a soup company to use the song as a jingle. We can retire on the residuals."

Eddie smiled. "Love it."

"Only one thing left to do."

"Write the song?" I asked.

Lucas put his arm around me. "We need to eat some soup. Get inspired!"

Chapter 8

Somersault

We sat at our usual round table toward the back of the club. I had a vodka mixer in hand. It hadn't been our greatest set. Lucas and Eddie couldn't find a balance of sound, and I was stuck trying to cater my beats to them. Either they were trying to out-play or out-volume each other. At least we got some people up dancing.

Eddie raised his glass and said, "To a good set."

"But much better drinks," Lucas responded. He turned to me. "What's wrong? You seem distracted, somewhere else."

I was, but I couldn't tell him why or he'd be upset. "Just out of it."

He nodded. "Well, I'm just going to come out and say it. I think we've performed better."

Eddie said, "They all can't be homeruns."

"But if we're going to make a name for ourselves, we need to kill it every time. Build a reputation."

"It's music, Lucas. Not homework." Eddie turned to me for support. "If you're not feeling it, then you're not feeling it. And if we want to build a reputation, then we need to stop changing our name and not waste our jam time coming up with new ones."

Lucas slammed his beer down on the table. "That's the dumbest thing I've ever heard."

"No," Eddie started, "the dumbest thing was when that guy who rented my extra room told you he always wanted to drive to Hawaii."

"Oh, yeah, that was really stupid, too. But I think he was high on cough syrup. What's your excuse?"

Eddie leaned forward and made a grunting sound.

I stood with my drink and said, "While you guys have the worst conversation ever, I'll be back in a bit."

Lucas grabbed my wrist, stopping me. "Where you going?"

"The little girls' room. Want to come?" Lucas looked like he was considering it. Last thing I wanted was him drunk, getting hot and heavy. "Actually, I take that back."

He smiled, then pressed his lips against the top of my hand and released it.

I walked past the bar, peering into the kitchen for Raymond on the way. I checked with the bartender, who said he was definitely supposed to be working tonight but he was not sure where he was now.

In the washroom, I balanced my drink

against the sink tap and looked at myself in the mirror. My hair was rockin' it with the purple tint and the new pink highlights I put in last night. I still looked good in my tight black pants and black Captain America tank. I'd noticed that my pants were a bit snug after the set and started tugging at them to loosen their grip on my thighs. I loved how all the gigs were great workouts, but they were probably not enough to work off the cals I had in drinks after. Maybe it's time to cut back on the drinks. I thought about trying to get through school and gigs without some liquid courage. I pictured Lucas's reaction to my going clean. I let out a laugh. Who was I kidding? I couldn't stop drinking even if I wanted to.

The washroom door swung open. It was Raymond.

"There you are! What are you doing in here?" I asked.

His face was all serious, almost sad.

I put my hand on his arm. "What's wrong?"

"Is there anyone else in here?"

I peaked under the stalls. "No. Just me."

Raymond took a slow step toward me. From his jacket pocket, he took an envelope and held it out to me. He looked like he was about to cry.

"You didn't get in?" I guessed. "I'm so sorry."

Then he flashed a big, bright-eyed smile and announced, "It worked! I got in to the George Brown chef program!"

"Oh my God! I'm so happy for you!"

"There's more. I'm getting the scholarship!"

I jumped up and down with him, bursting with excitement. "I'm so proud of you."

"It's because of you that I got in. Thank you, thank you, thank you!" He gave me a swinging, feet-off-the-floor hug.

The door swung open again. Filling the doorframe was Lucas.

Raymond took one look at Lucas's face and dropped me.

Lucas asked, jaw clenched, "So, kid, how long have you been sleeping with my girlfriend?"

"Lucas," I said, "come on. We're just celebrating —"

"Celebrating a Mexican loser getting into my girl's pants?"

Raymond shook his head, holding up his envelope. "It's not like that."

But I could see how it looked to Lucas. Girls' washroom, alone with me, Raymond hugging me. It looked bad.

I stepped toward Lucas to calm the tension in the small, three-stalled room. But he lurched forward, surprising a squeal of fright out of me. He passed me and barrelled into Raymond, football style, sending him crashing into the brick wall. I reached out for Raymond, trying to stop him from hitting his head on an automatic dryer that protruded from the wall.

Lucas lunged again at Raymond. "How long you been seeing her behind my back?"

Freaked out, Raymond shouted, "No!" He reached for the college acceptance letter that had fallen on the filthy bathroom floor. He was met with a fierce punch in the face from Lucas.

Raymond hit the ground hard. I tried to pull Lucas back as he kicked him repeatedly. But drunk and enraged, Lucas was too strong.

I screamed, "Lucas, please stop!" But the loud music from the other side of the door drowned out my voice.

My first instinct was to go get help, but I didn't want to leave Lucas alone with Raymond. I hoped the door would open. Someone. Anyone.

Nothing. I screamed again at Lucas, begging him to stop. He just kept delivering more hits. Blood splattered up from Raymond's face.

I fell to the floor. I crawled on my hands and knees toward Raymond. Tears flooded my face, and my body heaved with sobs. Finally Lucas stopped his attack and stepped back.

I bent over Raymond. He was bloodied. His nose was flattened. His right eye was swollen with a grotesque gash. He twitched sporadically.

Lucas picked me up by my arms. He dragged me away from Raymond and through the washroom doors. He took me out through a side door, to an alley. I tried to fight him, to stay with Raymond. But I was scared I would end up on the floor with him.

"Why'd you sleep with him? He's a frickin' dishwasher."

I screamed, "I didn't!" through tears and spit. "What's wrong with you?"

He grabbed my shoulders and squared me to him. "What's wrong with me is that I care about you. God, isn't it obvious?"

Chapter 9

Downbeat

Strangers eyeballed me.

I could barely keep it together on the streetcar. Images of Lucas beating on poor Raymond flashed in my mind, a series of stills set to replay. Why didn't I try harder to stop Lucas? Who was this guy I thought I knew? How could I have just left Raymond there? Was he okay and what would happen now? I had more questions than answers, and one inescapable burning point boiled and churned inside me. This was my fault.

Raymond trusted me and I trusted Lucas.

I got off at my stop and walked up my street, arms crossed around myself. I grunted when I saw the light on in my dad's bedroom. Key in the front door, then hand in the liquor cabinet, I was on autopilot. I grasped a bottle of I-didn't-care-what and snuck into my bedroom. I checked the marker line my dad drew on all his bottles. It didn't line up. Either it was old or my dad's been drinking lately. Whatever. I needed this. I took a swig and winced at the warm, sharp taste. I took another sip, followed by a few more. I could feel the drink push away reality. The pain, the fear, was dissolving and leaving me numb.

My phone lit up, catching me off guard. It was Eddie.

"Hello?" I said weakly.

"You're okay? I was worried. What happened to you?"

"I'm fine. Just wasn't feeling well so I got some fresh air."

"I was having my beer and Lucas went to talk with the manager. Then I heard a scream through the music. I came to check on you —" Eddie stopped, choking up.

Did Eddie know? What did he see?

"Olivia, I don't know how to say this . . . it was Raymond. He was attacked, badly beaten. He looked awful. The guys couldn't wake him up. They had to call an ambulance."

The floodgate of tears started again. My dad knocked on my door and creaked it open.

"Just checking you're home."

I pressed the phone against my chest and the bottle of booze against my leg, but he saw my tears before I could wipe them away.

"You okay?"

I nodded. But I was so not okay. "Can we talk tomorrow?" I said as calmly as I could manage.

He nodded and said good night before leaving.

"Olivia?"

"Yeah, Eddie, I'm here."

"Was that Lucas — never mind. None of my business.

"Is Raymond alive?"

"Yes."

The news was little comfort. "Do you know which hospital?"

"I overheard the ambulance driver say St. Michael's."

"And police?"

"Yeah. I'm just glad you weren't there to see it."

* * *

I tried to ignore my phone buzzing away in my pocket. I didn't have to check to know who it was. And the "it" was the last person I wanted to talk to. I was in Geography and couldn't answer anyway.

The night before, I'd had zero sleep, and questions continued to pound my brain. How could I focus on school not knowing how Raymond was? Should I go to the police before they came to me? Was it too late?

The teacher was droning on about the role of geotechnologies related to global warming. I wasn't in the mood to save the planet. I pressed my hand against the phone in my pocket. The damn thing wouldn't stop. Option one: turn it off. Option two: stop hiding from it.

Once the bathroom stall door was locked, I sat on the toilet, pants up, soaking up the only privacy available between 8:50 a.m. and 3:00 p.m. My phone was in my hand. It had been buzzing all day. The front screen was filled with phone alerts and texts.

I cleared the notifications from Lucas away. If only it would be that easy to make him disappear in real life. The what-to-dos and the what-not-to-dos battled it out in my head. What I really needed was some advice. My dad would know what I should do. But the fallout of his disappointment would not be worth the price of admission.

Enough, I decided. I pressed 9-1-1 into my phone. With my thumb on Call, I was startled when my phone went off. I swiped it, thinking I'd accidentally made the call. Then I heard a voice. Could 9-1-1 track me?

"Hello?"

It was Lucas.

"Olivia. We need to talk."

I put my thumb on the screen to end the call.

"Thought you had Intro to Psych, but didn't see you there."

He was trying to find me? I pictured him lurking on the university campus, looking for me among the hundreds of first-year students. What if he tracked my phone here? He'd kill me if he knew I was in high school.

It was only a few days ago that I thought Lucas was so cute and kind-hearted for giving me the big break to play in his band. He thought I had talent, and that made me feel so special. I was even seriously considering having sex with him.

He had sent shivers up my spine with a simple touch. And we had a great thing going with the band. The gigs were fun and I needed the practice. But after yesterday, after what he did to Raymond, the very thought of Lucas sent different shivers up my spine — shivers of fear.

"Where were you?" Lucas asked frantically.

I wanted to hang up, but that wouldn't stop the calls. "I'm in Convocation Hall. There's, like, eight hundred students."

He didn't respond. I had done my homework so well. It was something I used to be proud of. The plan to make them believe I was one of them had worked. But I never imagined leading the double life of two Olivias would be so hard. Olivia the high school girl was much easier to keep up. Just go to classes, fake interest and survive until 3:00.

"I looked for you."

"Well, I had a doctor's appointment."

"Really."

"Anyways, I don't have to tell you my whereabouts. After what you did, I don't owe you anything."

"You're still mad?"

"*Mad?* That word doesn't even begin to describe how I feel. You beat the brains out of an innocent guy trying to better his life."

"I'm sorry. Okay?"

"You can't just apologize for something like that."

"Olivia, don't you understand how much I care about you? How much I'm into you?"

His words stung. "Who cares about how you feel about me? Raymond is in the hospital because of you!"

"Don't talk to anyone about that."

"Eddie said the cops were called."

"If Raymond talks, there could be trouble for the both of us. But don't worry. None of this changes how I feel about you."

"Lucas, are you listening to me?"

"Yes. Of course."

"I can't be involved with someone with zero compassion. It's over. We're over."

"You can't. I love you."

"What? No, you can't love me."

"But I do."

"Us, you and me . . . it's over. Goodbye."

"Please don't hang up. Can I say one thing?"

"If it's about us . . . no." I waited. Last chance.

"God, I didn't want to tell you this, but someone at the bar was asking questions. I think it was Raymond's brother. He wants to know who beat him up. He said he saw you with Raymond that night."

"He never mentioned a brother —"

"That's because he's got a criminal record. I'm talking about drug dealing, gang stuff, like theft. I even think he's got a murder charge. I care about you and your safety. If you see anything, hear anything, you have to let me know."

I thought about how Raymond was trying to better himself. He was the complete opposite of his brother, I thought. And now he's battling for his life in the hospital. And it's all my fault for letting Lucas love me.

Chapter 10

Spinning

My dad insisted I go with him to the mall. I agreed because I figured if we were out in public, it would be harder for him to ask me about last night. I stayed close to him as we zigzagged the heavy foot traffic of the Eaton Centre. The centre was busy as always with worker bees flocking to get out and shoppers anxious to get in. We entered the bookstore, browsed the latest fiction and then purchased two Mocha Frappuccinos from the café.

While window shopping, my dad asked, "So, how are you doing?"

"Okay."

"Okay good? Okay bad?"

"Can we talk about something else?"

"I have to say, I'm worried about you, Olivia. I feel like I don't know anything that's going on in your life. You gotta give me something. How's the group assignment that you've been working on forever?"

We paused in the middle of the mall and stopped to watch the water fountain. The water shot up past us with great force.

"I quit the band."

"What? When?"

I shrugged.

"And the crush on what's-his-name? Lucas?"

"Dad! Stop with the interrogation!"

"I was just asking a question."

On the other side of the circular space, I caught a man looking at me. I'd usually credit it to some innocent eye flirting, but Lucas's warning surfaced. *Don't act paranoid, Olivia,* I told myself. But this guy looked familiar. Was it because he looked like he could be Raymond's brother?

He wore skinny black jeans with a silver belt keychain looped to his front pocket. Jet-black high-top boots matched his thick-zippered black leather jacket. Could Lucas be right? Was Raymond's brother following me? Could he have his gang friends looking for me?

I turned away, trying to keep him from catching a good look at my face.

"Olivia . . . hello?"

"Yes. Sorry, Dad. It's just a tough time, okay?"

"I understand. But it's normal for a parent to want to know why. Did something happen?"

Of course something happened! I sneaked a peek at leather-jacket guy. He was on the phone, still looking over the fountain in my direction.

I took the lead and my dad followed me into the safety of a women's clothing store. I found a discount rack at the very back and stood facing the front.

Still no sign of leather jacket.

All I wanted was to escape the mall and get someplace safe.

* * *

That smell. A mix of urine, awful food and chemical cleaners. As soon as you pass through the front doors of the hospital, it hits you hard.

I walked out of the elevator on the third floor and applied a double dose of foamy hand sanitizer from the container hanging crooked on the wall. The hall was quiet except for the sounds of machines beeping and whooshing. I followed the directions from the volunteer at the information desk and found Raymond's room: 1305 North.

It was the end of visitors' hours. The room

was dark except for the fluorescent bar that glowed a sickly white above Raymond's head. I approached him cautiously. His eyes were closed and there were tubes coming out of his nose. He had a cast on his left arm. I felt the tears that had been welling up trickle down my face. I had been there in the girls' washroom and did nothing. What's wrong with me?

Coward.

Up close, Raymond's face was many shades of purple, blue and green. I noticed the eyelids were swollen. I could see the gash near his eye was ballooned up, even though it was covered with a bandage. I gave him a soft kiss on his stony cheek and whispered, "I'm sorry."

Behind me, I heard the door handle turn. I lurched forward, taking cover behind a privacy curtain. I gripped it to stop it from swaying. Even if it was just a nurse, I didn't want anyone to start questioning who I was.

The voice on the other side was male and very clear. He wasn't talking English. Was it

Spanish? Was it the guy from the mall? Was it Raymond's brother?

I reached for my phone in my pocket. Maybe I could use Google Translate. But what if my phone went off? I carefully slid my right hand over it, flicking it to Silent.

I shuffled left to find an opening to look through. Then there was an itch. It crept up from my lip. *Oh no, a sneeze.* I tried to fight it back. As I turned away from the curtain, I suddenly noticed that there was somebody in the other bed behind me. An old lady made eye contact with me. She reached out for me like she was trying to ask for something.

Achoo!

I gasped, then froze like a sculpture. *Damn, damn, double damn.* The voice on the other side of the curtain stopped. Then there were more footsteps. I had no choice.

I sat down in the chair next to the old lady and explained that I was a volunteer visitor on rounds chatting with people. I introduced myself with a made-up name and asked her a few questions about how she was. I felt awful, like I was using her. But I could see the feet of the man talking to Raymond's sleeping form.

How long was he going to stay? One minute turned to twenty and I was running out of things to talk with this woman about. Finally I heard him walking away. Then the door closed. I said goodbye to the old lady and made my exit.

Chapter 11

Zombie

Wednesday night band practice. What's not to like? Some jamming, some out-on-a-limb songwriting, good time with friends and a few drinks. Not this time. I arrived with a plan to oust Lucas and make him pay for his crime.

I found Lucas in the shed on his phone, his guitar still wrapped in its case.

"Where's Eddie?" I asked.

He didn't look up. "Couldn't make it."

I didn't believe him. "The only reason I'm

here is to say bye to Eddie and grab my sticks."
I had this entire scene played out in my mind,
the words rehearsed to perfection. Step one:
arrive early to tell Eddie everything. Step two:
form a new band, no Lucas. Now what?

Lucas finished typing something before
turning the phone off. He started to walk
toward me. I felt ill just looking at him. "Since
there is no practice today, let's go get a beer.
Or something stronger. We need to talk. I miss
you and have been looking for you everywhere
on campus."

"No."

"One drink. It's on me, and you can leave
if you don't like what I have to say."

"You should see what you did to him."

"You saw him! Are you crazy? If Raymond's
brother found you, he'd do the same thing to
you or worse."

This was all way off my careful script. "No
one saw me."

"How do you know? You live in a pretty

innocent little world of textbooks and lecture halls. You don't know how these people work. You think they're looking for you at the club or at the hospital. But maybe they're following you on the streetcar. This is his brother we're talking about." Lucas reached for his jacket. "They could've followed you here."

"You're overreacting."

"Oh my God. How do I get you to see the reality? This is exactly why you need me to take care of you."

I moved toward the door. "Lucas, I'm going to the cops."

He responded with a big smile. "She's going to the cops," he announced, as though there were a crowd gathered in the shed.

"What's wrong with that?"

"I'm trying to treat you like the smart person you are. But I'm getting tired of breaking the news to you. We're both guilty. You're what is called an accomplice."

It couldn't be. I didn't push Raymond into

the wall. I wasn't the one throwing the punches.

He placed his hands on my shoulders and I cringed.

"I didn't want to tell you this." His voice had less volume, less bite. But it wasn't anything like kind. "Someone's been following me. I lost them to get here. But it's just a matter of time before they connect us. Raymond's brother, he has friends, and they're dangerous."

My mind raced. Was it skinny jeans? Or another member of the gang?

"When I told you that I loved you, I meant it. And I think it would be better, safer, if we stuck together. Once we get out of this, we can make great music together."

I wanted desperately to confide in Lucas, to believe in him again. But I hated him getting his way, having an answer for everything I said. I had only one option to get out of here a winner. I turned, removing his hands from me. "I quit the band, and I'll be back with my dad's car tomorrow to grab my kit. It better be here."

✳ ✳ ✳

Raymond. That's all I could think about. In period one, Art class, I started welling up, my breathing growing out of control. Deep sadness took hold of me.

I tried my best to keep it together by focusing on class work.

Be a good student.

Be a good girl.

In period two, Math, pencil in hand, I did whatever the teacher asked, and then some. Or I did it to the best of my abilities. A nice drink, even a sip, would've helped to calm my nerves. Without one, I tried hard to finish the worksheet.

By the time lunch hit, a massive headache had taken over and clouded most of my brain. Maybe it was all the concentrating on my work. Deep down, I knew it was because I still needed a drink.

My mind searched, like a rat in a dumpster. There had to be some booze somewhere. Unfortunately my search through my backpack and locker came up empty. Then I saw it.

Head craned into my locker, I squeezed. *Squirt.*

The taste was sharp and it felt like fire on my tongue. It burned down my throat and into my stomach. I slammed my locker shut, the inside of my elbow pressed against my mouth. I stopped at a water fountain, gurgled cold water and spat it out. It did nothing.

Never again, I told myself. Liquid hand sanitizer was not the answer.

On the way to my next class, I spotted a police officer entering the main doors with the principal.

Adrenaline started rushing through me.

I turned and took the stairs three at a time.

Please don't let me be arrested at school.

I kept moving, bursting through groups of students. "Hey, watch it!" I heard, and "What's your problem?" I kept going, like somehow there was safety deeper in the building.

In fourth period, English class, I sat in the corner, back against the wall.

Around me, people chattered, cracked jokes, completely stress-free. How could I have been so naive as to think I could've pulled it off? How could I pass myself off as a university student when I couldn't even pass high school? What was I thinking? How do I get out of this? With too many late-night gigs and all the lies about university, older Olivia was due for burnout.

Restless, distracted and scared, I couldn't sit still. I anxiously drummed air fills under my desk until the kids beside me starting to take notice. All class, I waited for the call. I was ready for the police to come and take me away. When the bell finally came, I darted out the side door and ran all the way home.

Chapter 12

Landslide

"Have a seat with me."

My dad sat in the front room, his arms folded. I was surprised to find him home in the middle of the day.

"How was your day?" he said, a bit too calmly.

I sat in the grey corduroy chair across from him. "It was okay, I guess. I had a prep period at the end of the day and decided to come home and do some work."

"Well, there's something we need to talk about."

My fingers and jaws clenched. Did he know about the police at school? Was he looking for a confession?

I watched as he scratched at his day-old stubble. "Did you work today?"

"I did a half-day."

My mouth was dry. My tongue felt like a slab of cement. I pictured the police officer behind him . . . waiting. It was the one from school, face behind dark shades, with a thick moustache, cuffs ready to take me.

My dad uncrossed his arms. "You need to be honest with me."

"Okay. Of course." I spoke slowly and deliberately as though sending the words over a minefield. One wayward word, and it could be *kaboom.*

"No more lies." He took a deep breath. "Guidance called. Now, why would they reach out to me?"

Guidance. No cops. Phew. Now to think of the answer. "My grades?"

"Yeah. A few of your teachers notified the guidance counsellor that you weren't completing your work. Worse, you were falling asleep in class."

He held his look. It was my turn.

"I'm sorry. I've been trying to do better." Even if today was the first day I actually did, at least it wasn't an outright lie. And thinking of my long list of lies, I figured it was minuscule.

"Okay," my dad started. "I'm glad to hear that you're aware of the issues and that you're starting to do something about it. But, I've gone ahead and booked a guidance appointment for tomorrow."

"What? Dad, I said I was trying."

"It's not just for you."

"I don't get it."

"I'll be there, too. It's important that you and your school know that I'm there. That I care."

I rubbed my eyes. My dad playing the

attentive parent was the last thing I needed.

My dad stood. "But that's not all. I've got something even more important to discuss."

Oh crap, here come the cops. I knew they'd track me down today.

He opened his liquor cabinet. He sat back down with a glass and a bottle and slowly poured himself a whiskey. Neat — no ice.

My mouth watered as he took a sip and then paused to admire the way the golden-brown liquid looked in the speckled glass. It was torture.

"You know your grandfather was a smart man."

"Abuelo Ernesto?"

"Uh-huh." He took another sip as I watched, agonized. "He came here barely able to speak English. But he was a street-smart man. Back in Cuba, he had a cart. He sold anything he could get his hands on. Then he got a store. And he worked nonstop. It didn't bother him — he loved it."

"Dad, I appreciate the story, I really do, but I have work to do."

"Let me get to my point. I'll be quick. My dad's one gripe was that people would steal from him. A little here, a little there. It added up. He eventually got good at trapping the shoplifters." He raised the whiskey bottle. "Take this, as an example."

Oh crap.

"He'd mark things like bottles of olive oil, bins of dried pasta and jars of candy to see what people swiped. I even got caught once taking some snacks from his store. It was my family's store, so I had thought, *Why not?* Big mistake." He pointed to a black marker line on the bottle of whiskey.

"The line doesn't match with the amount of alcohol. It's way off." He had me. Or did he? I stared at the markings on the bottle.

Then he said, "That's not how it works." He turned the bottle upside down. The line was clearly a few drinks — plus one — above the level of the whiskey, revealing just how much I had taken.

"Dad —"

"Olivia. I said no more lies. Almost every one of my damn bottles is off the mark."

I buried my face in my hands.

* * *

A prisoner in my own room, I turned on some music and lay down. I stared at the ceiling and let the music fill my room. How did I get to this point in my life? One moment, I'm proud of myself for having the courage, the guts, to bravely live my own life. Going against the humdrums that line the walls of high school. Then the next moment, I'm embarrassed by my terrible web of lies. Maybe I shouldn't have been so quick to criticize those humdrummers. What do they really have to worry about?

The music began to slowly seep through me, crashing through my negativity. I sat down at my Typhoon TYDD-01, put on my headphones and started jamming. Hard. Letting my body take out its frustrations. Sweat started building on my forehead. I was pounding away on my electronic drum kit. *Dratat tat tat tzzing ting.* I was attacking the beats when suddenly it dawned on me that there was someone I might be able to reach out to. Resting my headphones around my neck, I grabbed my phone and dialled.

"Olivia! Feels like I haven't heard from you in forever."

Eddie's voice was warm and welcoming. I didn't have to see him to know he was smiling. "Yeah."

"I was surprised when Lucas cancelled band practice. You okay?"

"Yes." I guess Lucas didn't mention I quit.

"Doesn't sound like it. Let me get somewhere more quiet . . . hold on a minute."

I folded my legs on my bed while I listened to the sounds emanating from his phone.

Some rustling, the chatter of people in the background. "You there?"

I opened my eyes. "Where are you?"

"Coffee shop, trying to get some work done. But it seems like everyone else on the planet is here, so I'm out front. So what's going on?"

"Nothing really."

"Yeah, right. I knew it was a bad idea for you and Lucas to hook up. Never mix love and business."

Love? Really?

"And never ever mix love with music," he added.

"Trust me when I say I don't love him."

"So I was right."

"It's complicated."

"Well, I can tell you you're the first girl he's really been into. I mean, in a serious way."

"How many have there been?"

"I don't want to talk for him —"

"Eddie, I need some advice."

"Okay, of course. Let's get together. How about a beer at that place on Harbord? Or maybe somewhere quieter for coffee?"

I stood to look out the window. The sky had clouded over, making it look later than it was.

"Olivia?"

"I'm thinking." I wanted to see him, but that meant finding a way out of here. And if I got caught . . . I don't even want to go there. But Eddie was offering the two things I needed most right now: a friend and a beer, or two, or three.

"Say yes."

"Yes. Scullers, upstairs in twenty."

I went to say good night to my dad in his room. I told him how exhausted I was and that I just needed to sleep it off. I promised that tomorrow he and I would go to the guidance department, and that there would be changes. I gave him a kiss on the cheek and pretended to get ready for bed.

Ten minutes later, I said good night again on my way downstairs "for a glass of milk." I walked past the fridge and out the front door.

It wasn't until I stepped onto the road that I felt a brief sense of relief and freedom. *Tonight first,* I thought. *Tomorrow is another day.*

Chapter 13

Fade Away

Blood pumping, I moved fast along the sidewalk. I took the curb past some slow students out for a stroll. Suddenly I heard a car do a double honk. I jumped back, a bit too close to the edge of the curve. I raised my hand, waving apologetically. Safely back on the centre of the sidewalk, the car honked again — the same two times. It seemed less of a *watch out* and more of a *hey you*.

Don't look back, I told myself. Once is a

fluke, twice is intent —

Honk-honk, honk, honk. Louder, longer. Now I was worried.

Had I been followed?

Don't look. Don't give them the advantage.

Up ahead, the cars and people on the busy street gave me my escape. There was a large café on the corner. I remembered they had a back patio. I could leave that way. My pace increased even though a large part of me wanted to stop. Just talk, apologize and reason with whoever these people are. I was on their side. I'm the one who helped Raymond get into chef school. But instead I found myself running.

Not long ago, I had been to that café with friends. That was before the band, before Lucas, before the drinking. Life was simpler then. I just played in the school band and I was an A student. All I'd had was a few drinks at a party and just a sip or two from my father's liquor cabinet.

Behind me, the engine revved. A rusted

white van with faded etching along the side entered my sight and jumped the curve. The driver's door opened and someone hurdled around the front. It was Lucas.

"Are you crazy?" I yelled. "You almost flattened me!"

"Olivia, they came for me." Lucas's usually wavy hair sat limp from sweat.

"Who?"

"Raymond's brother!" — Lucas's breathing was uneven — "and friends."

"What? Where?"

"The dorm door was open. I shouldn't have gone in. They were waiting — in the kitchen. Three of them . . . four of them, I don't know." He paused, eyes on the ground by my feet.

He looked like he wanted me to hold him, comfort him. No way. "What did they say?"

Lucas's eyes rose. "Nothing. They didn't have to say anything because one of them held a baseball bat. He probably used it to trash the place."

A group of teens were approaching loudly. They were big enough and there were enough of them that I could use them to get away from Lucas. I just had to wait until they got closer to us.

"But you escaped."

"Barely." He rolled up his sleeve. A bloodied cut zigzagged across his arm. "I practically rolled down the stairs to get away to my roommate's van in the alley. And then I saw you!"

"Where was your roommate?"

"Jesus, 'Livia, what's with the third degree? He lets me borrow his van when he sleeps at his girlfriend's. Don't you remember? We used it for the gig at South Paws last month. Lucas pointed to the faded lettering on the side panel: Cobb's Movers. It was impossible to make out the phone number. "Look, tell me you're not scared? Tell me you think I am crazy and I'll go."

I thought about the fountain at the mall

and the police at school. I'd be stupid not to be scared. Would the police be there with the principal tomorrow?

"You're actually being very selfish," Lucas continued. "I hate to be the one to break it to you, but here's the news flash. They probably saw pictures of you and me at my place. They know that you were playing with me that night. They saw you talking to Raymond. And the minute Raymond can clearly talk, you don't think your name will come up as a witness? And . . ."

"And?" I yelled, close to slapping him. "Maybe you're the one I should be scared of."

"And . . ." Lucas spoke slowly, spitting his words. "They find out where you live, too. Your dad innocently opens the door. And then they'll do to him what they tried to do to me!"

My head was spinning. I didn't know who to trust or what to do. How bad were these guys? "Lucas, you're asking for blind faith and that's hard right now. I want to see it. What they did to your place."

"What?" He was as surprised as me.

"I want to see your place. The mess they made."

"Are you crazy? Why would I ever go back there?"

"Because I want to believe you!"

"They could still have someone there, but if it's what you need . . ."

"It is."

"Olivia, I'll do it, but please think about just getting away until the heat dies down. Don't do it for me . . . do it for your dad."

Do it for missing the meeting with the guidance counsellor, I thought.

Lucas slid the van's side door open on squeaky rails. It was empty inside except for a box in the back corner. "There's more than enough space for the two of us to hang low. I'll sleep in front, you get the entire back."

That wasn't exactly a royal offer. If I had a dog, I'd feel bad about putting it in the back.

And anyway, I couldn't just run away. What about school? What would my dad think?

"You may not have feelings for me anymore, but I would never hurt you."

My hand reached for the passenger door. *Maybe we could just talk,* I thought. I could convince him it was not worth running away. If he turned himself in, the sentence might be lighter. A part of me just wanted to run away . . . even if it was with Lucas. It's not like anyone but my dad would miss me. School sucked, and right then, my whole life sucked.

So I sat there while Lucas climbed in the van. Where would we go? Only Lucas seemed to know. But maybe the police and everything else would go away.

Lucas passed me a beer, which I downed.

My dad would be pissed when he found me gone.

We took a curvy on-ramp and hit the highway. I looked out the side window and said goodbye to the Toronto skyline.

Looking at my phone, battery down low, I sent a text to Eddie.

have to cancel sorry

Chapter 14

Blur

The sun sliced through the trees, the light forcing me awake. I tried to prop myself up before I realized that I was already sitting in the passenger seat of the van. My surroundings came into focus as slowly as my old computer booting up.

Tightness in my neck made it painful to turn. My left arm lay asleep below the elbow. I wiped my eyes with my good hand and stretched. I noticed that Lucas wasn't in the driver's seat or the back of the van. I reached for the door handle and had to nudge the van door open. A wave of cold freshness rushed in and forced some of stale van air away.

Where was he? I called out for him and waited. Nothing. I couldn't come up with a single reason for him leaving me, so I decided not to worry. I had enough to worry about. My stomach growled. Rummaging through the back of the van for something, anything, I came up with nothing.

Where was he?

Where was I?

A quick check of my phone showed it was dead.

"You're up."

I turned, half-happy to see Lucas.

"Didn't want to disturb you so I went for a walk. Oh, found these." He held out some flowers he had obviously yanked out of the ground.

I took them, thinking they'd make the van feel a little less awful.

"How'd you sleep?"

I glanced at the van and then at him. "I would give a Yelp rating of negative two stars. These flowers, this whole thing . . . you know it means nothing between us."

Lucas smiled, raising both his hands out.

"I'm just saying," I continued. "Stating an unchangeable fact."

"I'm not reading into anything."

"So what's the plan? Tell me you have one."

"To lie low for a few days."

"That's it?"

"For now, yes."

"I don't have my phone charger or a change of clothes" — I pulled a twenty from my jeans pocket — "or much money. The van looks empty. What do you have?"

"I have what's most important: you here, safe from harm. The rest I'll figure out as we go."

"Do you even know where we are?"

"Why are you attacking the one person who's here to help you? You don't think I'm sacrificing a lot by being here?"

"Like what?"

"My whole life. I'm taking a chance on you."

"What do you mean!"

"My band is everything to me and I'm going places. I gave you an opportunity to go on that journey with me. But you're almost out of last chances and guess what? You could be the one in the cheap seats watching me on stage."

I could hear the highway cars and trucks rumble somewhere behind us. I might've been stuck here with Lucas, but I truly felt alone. I covered my mouth and shook my head.

"What's wrong?"

Tears rippled down my face as I looked for the right words to say. "This was a big mistake."

Lucas looked at me. His lips were pursed, eyes full of concern. In the glow of the morning light, he looked scarecrow thin, eyes shadowed in darkness.

"Olivia, this isn't the end. We will get through this. Maybe even write a great song about it!"

"We? Didn't you hear me? There is no we!"

He snarled before saying, "You might have given up on the band and music, but I plan on getting back to it as soon as possible."

"I hate you, Lucas" — tears persisted through my words — "and I wish I never knew you. I wish I never auditioned for your stupid band!"

"And I wish I never fell in love with you." He turned and trotted off, back toward the trees.

I flicked my hoodie over my head and returned to the stale warmth of the van.

Lucas appeared at the passenger door. "How about some spirits to uplift your spirits."

"What?"

He smiled and curled his index finger, signalling me to follow.

"I'm not in the mood for games."

"I promise you won't be disappointed."

I got up and followed him to the back of the van. The doors were open and a mishmash of half-finished bottles of alcohol were laid out above the bumper.

"Where did you get this?"

"You'd be surprised what was hidden where the spare tire was supposed to be." He guided me to rest on the top of the bumper. "First sip?" He handed me a bottle of Tanqueray. The alcohol set fire to my empty stomach. I could usually handle a drink or two of forty percent, but that was with the padding of food.

"Does it meet your expectations?"

I nodded.

"May I join in?"

I nodded again.

We moved onto the next bottle once that was done. Time seemed to lose meaning.

I said softly, "I don't like you," between sips.

"You're quite the woman, Olivia."

"And you know what bugs me most about you?"

He stepped back. "I'm not going to like this, am I?"

I got up and wobbled away from the van toward him. "You. All of you."

He grabbed his chest and stumbled back. "Your words strike like a knife." He stumbled back, begging, "One more sip before I die?"

"No!"

He pretended to drop dead on the grass and I laughed, hard. I turned to move back toward the van. Unfortunately, a moment later, he was back on his feet.

"And do you know what bugs me most about you?"

"Let me guess," I said, "everything."

"No. It's actually your eyes."

"What's wrong with my eyes?"

"And your lips." He pointed. "Yeah, definitely your lips, too."

"What!" I stumbled back to the van.

He followed. "Just look at them!"

I slapped his arm and followed with another sip of whatever was in my hand.

"Hey, if we're going to be honest . . ."

"You're so mean. What's wrong with my lips and eyes?"

"I'll tell you." He stepped closer. "They're too beautiful. I can't take my eyes off you." He leaned forward and kissed me.

"No!"

"Olivia . . . you worry too much. You can trust me. I'm here for you. I've always been here for you."

I was pressed against the side of the van. The world around me twirled, in a kaleidoscope kind of way. My hands dropped to my side and grasped the van for stability. Lucas, still in my face, was going at me with the determination of a woodpecker. I took a deliberate sidestep, toward the back of the van. Staying on my feet and pushing Lucas off my lips was harder done than thought.

Baby steps.

My hand on the break light was the signal that I was almost there. I heard the distant sound of glass. Must've been a bottle at my feet, but I'd never know with Lucas vacuumed to my face.

Bumper — I was almost there! All I wanted to do was lie down in the back of the van.

The combination of too much to drink and Lucas blocking my oxygen made it feel like I was on a roller coaster that wouldn't stop. The inside of what seemed like the van was warm. Lucas lay on top of me, smothering me. My eyes felt heavy. Would the spinning stop if I closed them?

Quick test.

No! Don't ever do that again.

The drinks that Lucas gave me seemed to be reversing direction, rising back up my throat. Maybe being horizontal was a bad idea. I pushed to get up, but couldn't. Lucas was on me. His hands snaked around every inch of me.

Was this it? My first time? I thought of all the romantic ideas I'd had about having sex with Lucas.

"Why are you laughing?" Lucas whispered too close to my ear.

Please throw up, I pleaded with myself. *Please throw up.*

Chapter 15

True Colours

As I woke up, I tried to scratch my way into the dark corner of mind to avoid my eyes opening. But open they did, one at a time.

"I thought you were dead." Lucas bent over me, one hand on my shoulder.

I wasn't in my bed, but in the van. My head and stomach pulsated with pain. Memories flashed back to haunt me. "Lucas."

"Yeah?"

I didn't know how to phrase my question.

"You're hungover," he said gently. "What you need is some fresh air." He opened the back of the van, letting in light and a windy blast of cool air.

I crawled toward the exit and took in the leftovers of the party scattered on the ground. Maybe I wouldn't have to ask the tough question if I picked up the drinking where I left off. "Anything to drink?" I asked.

"Do you know what time it is?"

I placed my palm on my forehead to pacify my growing headache. "I'm going to ask you something and I just want an honest yes or no."

"I wanted to and I think you did, too."

"Yes or no?"

He offered a superficial smile. "We didn't."

"Oh." That was good. "Because?"

"You threw up."

I searched for that memory.

"Everywhere."

"I'm sorry." Did too much alcohol save me

from Lucas? Thank God for drinking. There was little to celebrate, but if I hadn't thrown up, Lucas could've — would've . . .

"So today we need to move on," he said. "There are a few things we need, like money, food and gas . . . and a bathroom."

"What are we waiting for?" Anywhere was better than here.

We pulled into a place called Kettle Farm Foods beside a local gas station. I was able to clean up and grab a cheap five-dollar shirt to change into.

Now for the food. Country stores always have the best baked goods. Lucas told me to pick out a couple of fresh-baked pies. I enjoyed the warmth that filled my hands along with the pies. Lucas trailed closely behind an older man in blue overalls, big boots and green plaid shirt. Peering over a stack of jam jars, I watched Lucas knock elbows with the man, using his other hand to pull out a wallet from the back pocket. Lucas offered him a polite, "Excuse me," and approached me with a grin. "I prefer blueberry, but let's go," he said. He took the two pies from my hands and pulled me toward the cashier.

The woman at the cash was chewing gum and had a nametag that read "Val." "That'll be $19.80. And because you're buying two Kettle Farm pies, go ahead and pick out a third one. It's free."

I smiled. The more pie the better. "I'll get you a blueberry."

But Lucas said to Val, "Nah, it's okay."

She smiled, head at an angle. "Never seen anyone refuse a free pie before." Her follow-up laugh was fractured and crackly, like it hurt.

Lucas dropped a twenty-dollar bill down. "Keep the change."

While he guided me toward the van, I said, "We could've gotten another —"

"There's only one rule. Quick in, quicker out."

"You talk like you've done this before."

He didn't respond, focused on the old man's wallet. "Twenty bucks! Are you kidding me?" Lucas slammed his door shut and hit the gas, tossing the now empty wallet out the window before hitting the dusty road.

The aroma of strawberries and apples did wonders for the van. I couldn't take the anticipation anymore. Spork or no spork, this pie was a goner.

With pie filling everywhere, I silently thanked the man in the overalls and wished nothing but the best for him and his family.

Another twenty minutes down the road, Lucas slowed down. Out the window, I saw a gas station.

"Oh good." I held out my hands. "I need to clean up."

He continued past the station and stopped on the side of the road.

"You missed it," I said.

"Get out."

"What, here? No."

"I'll be right back."

I looked out at the empty brown field. "I don't believe you."

"I can't ask you to trust me . . . but trust me." He unclicked my seat belt and reached over to open my door. "It's got to be now."

I stepped out, hands still covered in pie residue. "Where do you want me to wait?"

"There's a tree." Lucas screeched away, pulling a tight U-turn. The passenger door swung shut on its own.

I hollered after him, "You're not going to rob the place, are you?" but he was gone. I stepped from a yucky patch of grass to one less yucky and took in my surroundings. What tree was he talking about? There was just grass going down to a roadside ditch. Farther down, there was just a field with a wire fence around it.

With arms stretched out and legs wide, I balanced my way down the ditch to a piddly-looking tree wedged against the fence. It took a minute before I realized I could wipe my dirty hands against it. I moved past it and stepped onto a rough boulder. Through a row of large bushes, I could see our van parked alongside a gas pump. On the opposite side, a woman was also filling up her SUV.

A large truck rumbled by. I turned away and covered my eyes as it kicked up little stones. When the dust settled, Lucas had returned. He pulled another tight U-turn and the door opened for me to get in. On his lap was a woman's purse, red with tassels. He rummaged through it. "Come on, come on."

"You got that getting gas?"

"I used the leftover five dollars to put a little gas in the van. This was a bonus."

"This doesn't feel right."

"No, but this does." He pulled out a roll of twenties. "There's over two hundred dollars!"

I didn't respond. Was this how it was going to be? Lucas and Olivia on a crime spree?

"This much money means we don't have to do it again. That SUV's gone. Let's go."

At the station, I cleaned up with actual soap and water, while Lucas filled the tank. Inside the store, we got some snacks, ice teas and a couple packs of gum.

Heading out, a man offered a polite, "How you folks doing?" as he held the door for us.

Lucas and I stopped when we saw the woman in the SUV parked in front.

She called out, "Yep, that's them, they took my purse." Before I could react, the man at the door grabbed me by my hair and tugged tightly.

I shrieked in pain.

The man said to Lucas, "There's nothing polite about taking a lady's purse, now is there?"

Lucas stood, fists clenched. "Let her go."

The man pulled me back harder and I cried out helplessly. "Give the money to him, Lucas."

Lucas looked at me and then at the man. He got the purse from next to the ice machine, where I'd made him put it. What use was her driver's licence and Costco card to us?

The man tugged my hair up so that I could only see down, like a dog. "Now give it to the lady."

Lucas passed it through the SUV's open window.

She looked through it, reached out and swatted Lucas hard on the head with it. "Where's the money?"

I winced as the man pulled even harder, his hands wrapped deep in my hair.

Lucas handed over what was left of the money plus the two bags of snacks.

The man released me. "I'm sorry if I hurt you," he said to me. "Just getting your boyfriend to do the right thing."

I nodded and looked at Lucas. Why wasn't he apologizing to these people? I moved to the van. "I'm sorry, too."

Lucas jumped in the driver's seat and sped away, taking his humiliation out on the van.

I took mine out on the gum.

Chapter 16

Don't

"Maybe we should turn back to the city?" We'd been driving around back roads for what felt like hours now.

Lucas looked at me like I was crazy. His eyes narrowed and he pursed his lips. "Another day. Then we'll see."

"Do you even have a plan? Where are we going?"

"North, if it makes a difference to you." He continued to drive.

There was little chit-chat and I was fine with that. I didn't feel like talking to someone who thought he could just take whatever he wanted and not care about who he might be hurting. I pressed my head against the window, wanting to be as far away from him as possible.

Then he said, "There's something really bugging me."

I barely turned to look at him.

"Us. I really want us to get back together. Like it used to be."

I had about a thousand razored responses to that, but he was driving and had my life in his hands. "Can we talk about it later?" I said.

"Yeah, but this trip has shown us how perfectly fit we are for each other."

"Trip? More like an escape from —"

"Hold it. You see that black Civic behind us?"

I squeezed over to see out the rear-view mirror. There was a black car quite a way back.

"Don't let them see you looking. I think

they've been following us the last half-hour or so."

"Could just be on the road." My seat belt locked tight against my chest as Lucas sped up. We were going fast, too fast for this two-lane road. "What are you doing?" I asked.

"You don't want to know."

"What?"

"Raymond's brother."

"Out here?"

"Gas station could've called the cops. These guys could be listening in. I had a friend who showed me. All it takes is a phone app. And look, they're still behind us."

I gripped onto the door handle. "Turn somewhere if you can."

"I have a better idea."

Lucas kept the van at thirty over the speed limit and then quickly slowed down after a curve in the road. He hit it into reverse and backed off the road into some trees, bending and breaking branches. Fifteen minutes of tense silence crawled by.

"What now?" I asked, nervously chewing on my last rectangle of gum.

"We spend the night here."

I should've expected that. I was getting irked by having to sleep in the dumpy, stinking van. I wanted to be in my bedroom. "If Raymond's brother is here, maybe the safest place to be is the last place they'll expect us. Home."

"Maybe. Don't know about you, but after that gas station, I could use a drink." He hopped out of his seat and into the back.

I stared at the keys dangling in the ignition. If I could get him outside, I could lock him out and take off. I could go home.

I touched the spot on my head where the man had grabbed my hair. It still hurt at the roots. Around me it was hard to tell what time it was because the trees covering the windows blocked out the light. Behind me, Lucas let out a large, "Ahhh," and then, "that's better."

I didn't feel like a drink. This whole thing was Lucas's fault. Let Lucas drink himself stupid. Then I can take off. He wouldn't know until he woke up.

Who was I kidding? I wouldn't survive another minute with Lucas, not sober.

"There's not much left if you want to join me."

I bounced out of my seat and into the back of the van. I wrapped my lips around the bottle.

"Better?" Lucas asked.

The drink warmed my stomach. I could feel it extending down to the tips of my hands and ends of my feet, numbing along the way. "Much." Couple more sips and I wasn't even bothered being in a van, surrounded by trees on some road.

Lucas sat with his back against the opposite side of the van. Our legs ran side by side, touching. "How's your hair? Lose any?"

I let another sip vacation in my mouth.

"Think so. He was pulling so hard I thought I was going to black out."

"I wanted to punch him in the face."

"You have some serious anger issues." The words slipped out of my loose lips.

He looked at me and then broke into laughter. "I know."

I broke out into a boozy snicker, too. Guess there was no way I was driving off in the van. The last thing I needed on my already growing record was a DUI.

"But you know," Lucas started, "even in the dim light of this old van, you look beautiful." He sat up and reached for my hair, stroking it. "I'm glad you're okay."

Our eyes locked. The tension in the van was as thick as mud. I pulled away. He let go of my hair and I covered the moment with a stretch.

"Sleepy?"

"Little."

He propped closer and ran his fingers through my hair again. I didn't want it to feel good. Then he leaned into a kiss.

"Don't."

"Come on. I love you." He moved to my side of the van and we were shoulder to shoulder. "Sit back," he said.

I didn't, until he handed me the bottle. I reached for it, but he didn't let go of it.

"What?"

"Promise me one thing."

Jeez. Now I really wanted that damn drink. "Maybe."

"Don't throw up this time." He did a bad job of trying not to crack up.

I smiled and grabbed the bottle from him. In the middle of a make-him-go-away swig, I felt Lucas's hand riding up my leg. Another sip and he was kissing the side of my neck. "Lucas!"

He pulled back a little. "Just drink some more. Trust me."

His hands were all over me. I thought about screaming, but who'd hear me? Fear cascaded down my body and his face felt coarse against my throat.

Then he rolled onto me and my fear turned into a panic attack. He had me pressed down and I couldn't move. I felt one hand on my zipper and another up my shirt. He attacked my bra, twisting and turning it until it unclipped. His hands were fumbling at the button on my jeans. *Enough!* I pushed his chest back. "Please stop."

"Let's have more to drink."

No amount of alcohol could rescue me from this. Trapped, I started to cry. Lucas started thrusting his hips against me.

I had to escape. But I couldn't break free. It was like I wasn't there anymore.

"Lucas. Get off. I have to pee."

"Hold it."

"I really have to go!"

He didn't respond. I wished I actually *could* go. That would stop him, just like my throwing up had.

This was not happening. Not here. Not now. If pushing and pleading wasn't working, I needed something else. A realization surfaced. The one thing I hadn't been with Lucas was honest.

"Wait. There's something you need to know . . . I lied to you."

He paused, barely for a second.

"I'm not eighteen. I don't go to university. I'm only sixteen."

"Ah-ha. Well, I like younger girls."

"You don't care? I lied to you. I'm just a kid! Let me go!"

"No. I love you."

I tilted my head and saw the back door of the van. I reached for it, but it was too far. I tried again, forcing my fingers into a full stretch until I touched it. I took a deep breath and reached with my right hand to grab onto the latch. I pulled down.

It opened.

Wriggling like a fish out of water, I freed

myself enough to slide out from under Lucas. I got to my knees and went for the opening, but Lucas grabbed onto my ankle. I clawed my way forward, dragging Lucas half out of the van with me.

"Let me go!" I screamed.

Kicking my foot loose, I stepped onto the grass and slammed the door shut . . . on his face.

He cried out in pain.

Through a blanket of tears, I steamrolled through a criss-cross of branches to get my purse from the front seat. Breathing out of control, I fought my way through the heavy greenery and away from the van. I didn't know where I was going or if I could find a road. But I did know that Lucas was behind me.

Chapter 17

Dark Star

My feet splashed in the mud-soaked ground, wetness soaking through my boots. Branches whipped back at me as I pushed my way through the forest. I kept my eyes down on the ever-changing ground. Around me, darkness made every step hard to land.

I thought about stopping, hiding against a rock. But the thumping of my heart, the whimpering of my cry and the hoarseness of my breathing would give me away. *Keep going,*

I ordered myself, *don't stop*. And no matter how fast and far I ran, the deep, dark forest seemed never-ending.

A loud crack rang through the air. I screamed before stopping. Heaving in air, I tried to quiet myself down enough to listen — to locate the sound.

There was silence.

I yelped as a faint sound rumbled in the distance. I was worried about dangers ahead. There were now flashes of light to accompany the sound. Run or hide? I saw a car and yelled out with as much enthusiasm as I could muster.

I repeated the words loudly, "Stop, stop!" I continued to wave my hands, hoping the driver would see me. *Where there's a car, there must be a road,* I thought.

Then in the same instant, the wall of trees came to an end and the headlights turned into red tail lights.

I collapsed onto all fours. My body was

overheated from the running. I was exhausted. The only glimmer of light was that I was free from the forest and I had a road to follow.

I got back on my feet and looked around. I decided to walk in the same direction as the car. Hopefully it wasn't leaving town.

I was alone on the two-lane highway. My stomach grumbled. Free from Lucas but without a game plane, I was scared to death, which was fine because I'd probably die out here. Should I have given in to him? Was I better off with him? He was a ticket home. I looked up to the cloud-filled sky and wished I could see the stars.

Step by damn step, I pressed forward. At least I hoped it was forward. The only signs I had were the ones on the side of the road. Instead of "Downtown next exit" or even an H for hospital, all I got was "Caution, curve up ahead." I walked for hours in the dark and the rain, sticking to the road, before stopping to rest.

A rumble in the distance caught my

attention and I sat up to listen. I must have fallen asleep. Headlights appeared. Do I wave it down or hide? It could be Lucas or Raymond's brother. It was coming. Time to make a move, but I couldn't decide. What if it was help? Like a total idiot, I froze.

The pickup truck sped by. It wasn't either of them. I should've stopped it!

I turned, head down and defeated. Stupid, stupid —

Bright red brake lights lit the darkness followed by little white reverse lights. The truck backed up. The passenger window was rolled down and a woman with fiery red hair looked out at me. "Now this is something I've never seen before. Are you okay? — never mind. I take that back. Are you alone?"

I nodded my head.

"If I open the door, some boyfriend isn't going to jump out of the woods?"

I shook my head and heard the door click unlocked.

"Let me give you a ride."

As much as I wanted to jump in, the last person I needed to trust was a complete stranger. I hesitated. *Think, Olivia.*

"Listen," she said, "a girl, alone, out here. It's much safer in here." She paused. "You can trust me."

The pickup truck looked warm and dry. "Where am I?" I asked.

"Nowhere, really." She smiled. "But we're heading to a town called Lakeview. Only there's no lake. Don't you hate that?"

I didn't respond.

"There's a diner that I work at."

I reached for the door and entered the truck.

"My name's Darlene."

"Olivia." I closed the door and found the seat belt.

Darlene was humming along to something on the radio.

"Now you tell me, are you hurt at all?"

"No."

She reached behind me and held out a bottle of water and a granola bar.

"Thank you."

She pulled onto the road. "Sure is lonely driving out here at the crack of dawn. Usually I see the odd animal out here, not a young person. Anyways . . ."

Heavy eyes, sore limbs . . . *Don't you fall asleep again, Olivia, don't you dare,* I tried to tell myself.

* * *

I woke up, startled to find myself in the pickup truck. The sky was dark and gloomy and the lights were off.

"You're awake."

I turned to see Darlene.

Why did we stop? I slipped off a blanket that was wrapped around me.

"Be honest with me?" she asked.

Honest about what? How long had we been stopped? I reached for the door handle but it was locked.

"How old are you? Really?"

"Unlock the door."

"My girl, it doesn't take a mind reader to know you're in trouble. You were on the side of a remote road in the middle of the night. So the kind of trouble you're in must be the way-over-your-head kind." She scratched her chin. "You're what, sixteen?"

All I wanted was out. I'd find someone else who could help me. One with not so many questions.

I saw the handle on my door flick unlock.

"Let me help you." She pointed, palms still gripped on the steering wheel. "See that?"

I hadn't noticed that we were in a parking lot. I looked at a diner.

"That's mine. Let me get you something to eat."

That decided it. I nodded and we walked

toward the diner. Chimes sounded when the door opened. The lights flicked on and we entered.

She put on an apron that read "What's Cooking?" and stood behind a U-shaped counter with red stools. There were a few tables, and old-style booths lined the walls.

I saw a phone on the wall behind the counter. "Can I make a call? Even if it's long distance?"

She nodded, moving toward the kitchen. I dialled. "Dad."

"Olivia!"

"Dad —" I broke out into hysterical crying.

"Are you okay?"

I cried some more. A lot more.

"I was so worried you were —" He stopped, unable to get the words out.

I managed to get the crying under control, sort of. It was the greatest relief to hear his voice. I imagined clouds parting, symphonic music playing. "I'm so sorry. I really screwed up."

"Whatever happened, it doesn't matter."

"Have you noticed anyone following you? Anyone at the house?"

"No. I haven't seen anyone."

"Please, be careful. Someone's coming after you to get to me. It's a long story, but —"

"There hasn't been anyone."

"Are you sure?"

"Yes. Where are you?"

"Lakeview." I looked at a nearby menu. "The Countryside Diner."

"You stay put. We're coming to get you."

I put the phone down. The menu looked good. Too bad I couldn't afford anything on it.

Darlene called out from the kitchen, "Everything okay?"

"My dad's on his way."

"Okey-dokey. Washroom's over there."

I looked in the mirror in the washroom. My hair was a disaster. My face looked like it felt, like I was wearing a mask of dirt and tears. I washed up and knew I should feel lucky to be alive, but I just felt awful.

I sat at a booth. Darlene surprised me with a mug of hot chocolate and some pancakes with slices of fresh fruit on the side.

"I can't afford —"

"Oh, no worries. Just eat up."

I thanked her and took a sip of the hot chocolate. It felt perfect. "Mind if I wait here?"

"Not at all." She looked at me. "But you can't just appear at the side of road and not expect me to ask what's up, darling?" She leaned against the top of the booth in front of me, chin resting on her hand. "So. Shall I start?"

I didn't say no.

"Okay, the way I see it is that you're from a bigger city. First guess might be Kingston. But something tells me it's much bigger. I'm going with the Big Smoke, Hogtown. Toronto. How am I doing so far?"

I gave a nod.

"Good. I'd say you're no older than high school age. Old enough to drive, not old enough to drink or vote. The pressing question is, what would bring you all the way out here? Alone, soaked to the bone, penniless, scared as a lost kitten." She paused to roll up her sleeves. "I'd wager that you're on the run."

I bit into the first pancake. "How'd you know I was from Toronto?"

"The way you talk and move. Not a bad thing, just different from around here. Americans are my favourite to pick out. You see, around here, I'm Starbucks, Tim Hortons, Second Cup and Dunkin' Donuts all wrapped into one."

The door chimed and Darlene sighed at me. "My, my, we're off to an early start today."

We both turned at the same time as she said, "Welcome."

She stopped.

So did I.

Lucas stood at the door. A jagged cut smothered in dried blood ran across his forehead.

Chapter 18

Sabotage

Lucas slid into the bench in front of me. He told Darlene that he'd have a BLT with extra bacon and extra fries.

"My cook doesn't get in for another hour. Plus, sandwiches are only on the lunch menu. I do have pancakes —"

"Then I'll have whatever she's got, times two."

Darlene's eyes were doubtful. She didn't seem to want to leave me alone. "So that's a double stack of pancakes . . ."

"What's the issue . . ." He read her nametag and said her name in two parts: "Dar-Lene?"

She continued, "And two hot chocolates."

Lucas said through teeth clenched, "Just do your job and fetch the food."

I thought she was going to swat him with the menu. Instead, she turned to me. "What about you, sweetie? How are you doing over there?"

She wasn't talking about the food.

I didn't respond, but she saw the look in my eyes.

Lucas dabbed his cut with his finger. "And some of those hand wipes. Like a handful."

Darlene stepped to the counter.

"So this is awkward," Lucas said to me.

I didn't know what to say.

"Well, let's just say what we are thinking. I'll go first," Lucas said as he reached for a mini container of cream next to the ketchup. "I'm disappointed and I feel betrayed. I changed my life to protect you. I found the hero I could be inside."

"You were pushing for sex."

"Maybe. Is that so wrong?"

"You can't just take it! And I told you I was sixteen."

"And I told you I love you."

"And that makes you a hero?"

"I've never loved anyone before. And that makes you my girl."

He smiled.

How could he smile? "What about what I want?" I asked.

"You mean, what *we* want?"

"Lucas, I'm tired and I want to go home."

He slammed his hands down on the table, hard, sending the forks, knives and my plate hopping off the surface. "Where's my food, lady?"

Darlene arrived, easily carrying two large plates and a large mug. She glanced at me while putting them down. She returned to the counter, and I said softly, hoping to calm Lucas, "I'm sorry for hurting you. I didn't mean to."

"And I'm sorry for loving you. I did mean to." He dove into his food, the way I had done to mine.

I could see now how, in the beginning, I might have led him on. I thought Lucas was the answer to my prayers. Lucas was my ticket to a music career. Lucas was my escape from my reality. And later, when I got in the van with him, I put him in the driver seat of my life. Now, I wanted the steering wheel back.

"You tried to get me drunk in the van so you could get what you want from me. And you almost got it. That's not love. And that's not a relationship, and you know it!"

"We've got a long way to go before we're out of this mess. But then, everything will be great."

He couldn't see the truth. No matter what

I said, he still couldn't see how wrong this all was. My eyes rose to the cut below his hairline. "Does it hurt? It looks bad."

He shrugged, tough-guy like.

"You should probably see a doctor."

"I'll survive."

"Or at least clean it in the washroom." Maybe that was one way to get rid of him.

He looked at me, quietly chewing. "Don't let her take my hot chocolate away. And don't you go anywhere, either."

And just like that, he was gone.

In an instant, Darlene was at my side. She said in a hushed tone, "That boy is scary. We need to get you out of here immediately."

I slid out of the booth. "Where do I go? What do I do? He's just going to find me again. Darlene, please help me!"

She put her arm around me.

"Please call 9-1-1."

"I will, but this ain't Toronto. Douglas and Victor might take some time to get here, depending where they are."

Lucas's voice rang out of the men's room. "That's better," he said, as if to remind me of his presence.

Darlene spoke more quietly. "Maybe we just make him think you've taken off."

"Huh?"

The washroom door opened as I jumped the counter and curled into a ball underneath its ledge.

"Where is she?" Lucas asked angrily.

"She took off," Darlene said.

"Where the hell did she go?"

"Your guess is as good as mine. She was pretty scared."

"Hey, I'm not stupid, and I'm going to —"

"What? Continue to hurt people? Take advantage of young girls? Use them and threaten them if you don't get your way? What are you going to do?"

I heard the sound of a chair crashing across the restaurant.

"Well, I guess I'll do that for starters. And you have more chairs."

"I've called the police."

All I could see was Darlene's legs.

Lucas's voice grew louder as they stepped toward the counter. "Don't make me throw more stuff. Like this."

"It's just a container of sugar. Replaceable, like you."

I suppressed a shriek when I heard a glass container crash to the floor and shatter.

"Young man, you're going down a road that you can't return."

"And what about this?"

"Replaceable."

"Good to hear."

Another glass container hit the ground and broke into small pieces. Then another. And another.

"Replaceable. Replaceable. Replaceable."

I heard a hard thud on the countertop above me.

"Are you replaceable, too?"

It was Lucas. The countertop above me shuttered and creaked as Lucas stomped on top of it, pacing left and right. With each turn, he kicked something else to the ground. All around me were small explosions as salt and pepper shakers broke.

"Is the show over, Lucas? Clearly, she isn't here." Darlene's voice was firm.

"Yeah, you're right. What do I owe you for the pancakes and hot chocolate?"

"It's on the house."

"That's very generous, especially considering there were two hot chocolates."

"Well, you leaving is payment enough."

I curled closer against the back of the counter when Lucas jumped off it in front of Darlene. His boots appeared in front of me.

She cried out, "Please don't hurt us!"

"Us?" Lucas asked.

Then there was silence. The boots turned and I screamed as Lucas crouched and his face appeared in front of me.

He grabbed me, pulling me from my hiding spot. Like the man at the gas station, he had me by my hair.

"I gave you chance after chance, Olivia. Now it's over."

Chapter 19

Creep

Lucas's hands scratched my skin as he dragged me out. "Let me go," I squealed. "You're hurting me."

"This is all on you, Olivia," Lucas said.

Darlene, still behind the counter, shouted out, "I've called the police." There was a tremble in her voice, one I hadn't noticed before. I knew she hadn't had time to call the police. But did Lucas buy it?

"Shut up!" Lucas turned to me, still

gripping on to keep me in place. "All you have to do is stick with me, and all of this goes away."

"Okay, Lucas," I cried, "I love you. Let's get back in the van and just go. Stick to the plan." I'd say anything now to keep safe. I hoped my father was on his way.

"Do you really mean it?"

I twisted my neck to look him in the eye.

His face glowed red. "I made my feelings clear from day one. I don't know what I did to deserve the things that you did to me. Am I really that bad a guy for making you part of my band and protecting you against creeps like Raymond?"

"No, Lucas. This isn't even about you. Or us."

"What's that supposed to mean?"

"We shouldn't even have met. It's my fault for starting this."

"I don't understand."

"I live at home with my dad. The only

boyfriend I ever had was in grade seven. I go to high school. I'm the wrong girl for you."

Lucas didn't respond. I couldn't figure out what he was thinking, what his next move would be. He finally spoke. "You know, you act like you're above me somehow. Better than me. I spotted your talent. Helped you buy a kit, brought you in on the gigs. I didn't ask for all this."

I had one more card to play. "Lucas, we have to get out of here. Raymond's brother could be coming."

He looked at me with surprise on his face. After a long pause, he said, "Okay."

We moved toward the front door. I asked a question that was more for Darlene than myself. "Where are we going to go?"

"Not sure. But don't worry, I'll figure it out. But first stop is the dorm to pick up my guitar."

The chimes rang as he opened the front door. I turned back to Darlene and waved. She didn't look happy with my decision to leave. I felt some relief when I saw a phone in her hand. Maybe the police would track us down.

"Come on," Lucas called, "I think I passed Raymond's brother's red SUV on my way here."

I stopped. Raymond's brother's SUV. Why didn't that sound right? "You said Raymond's brother drives a black car. A Civic."

"Yeah. That's what I just said."

I stopped and thought about my phone conversation with my dad. He said no one had been by the house or bothered him.

"What's wrong now, Olivia?"

Why would Lucas go back to his dorm? I searched my memory for any sign that there really had been someone following me. All I could remember was Lucas scaring me with the idea of Raymond's brother wanting revenge. And him doing it every time I wanted to reach out to someone else.

"Oh my God." How stupid could I have

been? "There is no brother!"

Lucas held the diner door open. "Come on. I love you. Let's go!"

Lucas had lied just to keep me tied to him.

I screamed, half in terror and half in anger, "You made me leave home for nothing!" I backed up and he followed. The chimes sounded again. We were back in the diner.

"It wasn't for nothing. It was for us. And I know that deep down you still love me."

"Shut up!"

He pushed toward me.

I back-stepped to the counter and Darlene. "I could never love someone who can treat people this way! And I'm not just talking about me." My rage took over. I couldn't keep up the act anymore. I held my hands out. "Just look at this place!"

Darlene said, "Honey, this may not be the time for complete honesty."

Lucas inched up to my face.

I had seen him as a charismatic lead singer

of a band. Now, finally, I saw through him completely.

My voice cracked as I fought to hold back my mishmash of emotions. "What more do you want from me?"

Lucas looked at me. His eyes were wide and his lips twitched. He made several attempts to speak, but no words came out. Then he turned and walked out the door. He was gone.

Chapter 20

Breathe

All was quiet. The diner was a mess, shattered glass everywhere. Where would Lucas go? Why did I care?

Darlene said, "That was too much entertainment for one morning. Let me just say, I couldn't be more proud of you." She came to me and gave me a hug.

I started to cry. "I'm sorry about your diner."

"Oh, it'll be quite the cleanup, but it'll get

done." She pulled away so I could see her and said, "Listen to me. Don't you dare make this your fault. He had issues. You didn't know."

"Well, I can't help but feel guilty."

Darlene used a rag to wipe the counter before pouring me a glass of juice. "Sit."

I joined her at the counter.

"No one has the right to control what you say, think or do." She turned to the kitchen and cracked four eggs into a frying pan.

"You don't need to do that."

"It's not work to me." She laid strips of bacon into another pan. They sizzled on contact.

"How did I not see this coming?"

"Because you wanted to believe in the relationship too much. Trust me, you're not alone. All of us do it." She flipped the eggs. "The truth hurts, don't it?"

"Yes."

"The hard part is that you're not his first and you won't be his last."

"How do I stop him?"

"I've put a call into the police. I say we sit and eat."

A plate of food arrived. The eggs were soft and the bacon was crispy. The toast was somewhere in between. We both ate in silence for a while.

"You're worried about him, aren't you?"

"Yes. Stupid, I know."

"That feeling will stay with you for a bit. But don't let it tie you down." Darlene used a toast triangle to scoop up some eggs. We heard the door chime. Turning around, I was happy to see two police officers.

"Hi, Darlene. What happened?" the taller one asked.

"We had an incident. Mind your step."

"This is the Douglas and Victor I was telling you about," she said to me. She turned to the two men inching around the broken glass. "This is Olivia."

They wrote down my name and asked me how I was doing.

Darlene jumped in. "She was travelling with a young man. He's the one who made this mess before taking off."

"Olivia, you're going to need to come with us. We're going to need a full description plus anything else you can tell us about the person you were travelling with. Then we will get you home."

"Actually, I spoke to my dad. He's on the way here."

"Then we'll call him from the car and have him pick you up at the station. Okay?"

I nodded.

Darlene smiled. "They'll take care of you. You go on, now."

I gave her a big hug and told her that I'd never forget what she did for me. I paused at the door. "I don't know how to thank you. I'm so sorry for everything."

Darlene smiled at me. "Just get home safely."

* * *

Warm steam lingered in the air. I reached out
and wiped a section of the mirror clear with
my hand and looked at the reflection. The girl
staring back was not the girl I knew.

I was different. And it wasn't just being
clean and refreshed. Gone was the Olivia who
was sixteen and scared. I felt older, hopefully
wiser and definitely jaded. There weren't two
Olivias anymore. Just one. Me. I went into my
bedroom to get dressed.

I pressed my nose against my sweater and
breathed it in. At least that smelt like old me.
I sat on my bed and rubbed my hand along
my duvet. I stared out the window at the great
big world I used to wonder about. As I left my
bedroom, my feet enjoyed the comfort and
warmth of the soft carpet beneath them.

Music streamed through the house; a
guitar strummed and a raspy harmonica called
out. Descending the stairs, I saw Dad on the

couch. He had a coffee in hand and his socked toes tapped to the music.

As I stepped onto the main floor, the hardwood squeaked, announcing my arrival.

"You okay?" my dad asked.

I nodded.

He smiled at me.

"What?"

He pointed to my leg. I hadn't noticed that my left foot was stepping to the beat.

"Coffee or tea?"

"Peppermint tea, please?"

"Coming up."

He was playing it cool, casual. I appreciated it. The last thing I needed was the hard push of the law: I didn't want him to say I told you so. I already knew it was so.

From the kitchen, he said, "Are you ready for tomorrow?"

"Think so." I sat down on the couch and allowed it to absorb me. I will never take softness for granted again. On the coffee table in front of me, I noticed a white album was open. My parents' wedding album. There they were. My mom and dad, smiling, happy. They just fit together perfectly like connecting puzzle pieces.

"It was a beautiful day. Picture perfect, literally," Dad said as he returned with a mug of tea and some shortbread cookies.

The cookie dipped in the tea comforted me.

"I was thinking about you playing in a band," my dad said, "but you should consider singing yourself."

"Never saw myself as the singer type."

"Well, you express yourself so well with the drumming. If you get inspired to write some songs, adding vocals would make you the complete package."

I had some more tea and we both stretched out on the couch.

"So you met Eddie."

"Yeah. He just knocked on the door.

Found the address online. Then he told me what he thought happened to you. He's a good guy."

I nodded.

"A little too old for a high school student." My dad smirked.

I did, too.

After a full charge, I turned my phone on. In among the texts and calls from my dad and Eddie was one from Lucas.

"Everything okay?" my dad asked.

"Lucas texted me. Two days ago. It's a video." My dad leaned in as I touched Play. *What could it be?*

The video started close up on Lucas. He was in the van and his hair was a mess. He spoke quietly. "Hi, Olivia. It's pretty early in the morning. I couldn't sleep. Unlike you, who can sleep through anything." He turned the video to show me, fast asleep.

His voice continued off screen. "You're so beautiful. How do I deserve someone like you?"

The camera focused on his face again. "I know things aren't easy right now, so I got you a gift. It's nothing really, but I hope you'll like it."

He cleared his throat and began to sing softly.

It was our first real love
You got me so worked up
But waiting for you, maybe it got too much
Anyway, I wouldn't give you up
Like a prisoner in my mind, enthusi-
astic love's not kind . . .

He slowed the tempo for the chorus and fought back a tear.

Call it a wrinkle in time
Call it what you want
I'm just here for you
And yeah, I know I'm not so super cool

Just here to make you happy
If happy is what you want
Then it's what I want, too

He paused and smiled, caught in a moment of rare shyness. "That's all I have for now. I'm passing it on to you. It needs your talent, your words. It needs the special touch and groove that only you have."

I looked at Lucas, frozen on my phone screen. I thought about him and admitted to myself how much I fell for him. At least one side of him. The guy who gave me a shot and who was so supportive of my musical career. But then, there's the other side. The cold-hearted guy who hurt other people and didn't think twice about lying to control me. Lucas was messed up and I leapt right into his tangled existence, letting alcohol blur the lines between right and wrong.

"You okay?" Dad asked.

"I don't know," I cried out.

He wrapped his arm around me.

"I thought I wanted to be older . . . be someone different. Playing clubs, skipping school and drinking. But . . . that's not being older!"

"Olivia, look at me."

I wiped the tears from my eyes. "What?"

"You don't need to be older to be talented, to go after your dreams. And it might not seem it now, but all along, you were older than Lucas in every real way."

Epilogue

With the microphone pressed against my lips,
I almost expected the full sound of Lucas and
Eddie to kick in. I looked out at the quiet high
school audience. I was wearing my flowing white
flowered tank and my black leggings. I looked
respectable, with some soul. My hair was back to
its regular colour but in a short Afro.

I pulled my drumsticks from my back
pocket and held them up. "My name's Olivia
and this is my story."

I sat on a black stool in front of my Ludwig Breakbeats drums. I started with the high-hat, tapping it with my right hand and silently counting in fours. Then I pushed down on the pedal, throwing in some kicks to give a deep beat. With my right stick gently tapping on the snare drum, I found my tempo and began to sing the song that Lucas started.

It was our first real love
You got me so worked up
But waiting for you
Maybe it got too much
Anyway, I wouldn't give you up
Like a prisoner in my mind
Enthusiastic love's not kind

Call it a wrinkle in time
Call it what you want
I'm just here for you
And yeah, I know I'm not so super cool

Just here to make you happy
If happy is what you want

I switched from singsong to a sweet-tempered flowing rap.

That's how easy it is to get into the trap
I thought I knew the club scene, me at sixteen
Didn't
I thought I knew how to drum drunk
Didn't
I thought I knew me inside and out, up and down
Didn't
I needed to be free
He thought only of he
He started getting mean
Put my heart on the shelf

And I was alone, all by myself

Call it a wrinkle in time
Call it what you want
I'm just here for you
And yeah, I know I'm not so super
cool
Just here to make you happy
If happy is what you want

I returned to rapping.

That's how easy it is to get into the
trap
I thought I knew what it was like to
be cool
Didn't
I thought I knew everything and all
that
Didn't
I thought I knew how to be a good
friend, girlfriend and daughter . . .

Didn't

But you're my dream come true, he'd
say
His eyes a blazing blue
Will you please be my girl
I want to stay with you
But how can someone so mean
Ever be the answer to her dream

Call it a wrinkle in time
Call it what you want
I'm just here for you
And yeah, I know I'm not so super
cool
Just here to make you happy
If happy is what you want

My love, it's all too much
and it's so hard breaking up
Although we cannot be
It'll always feel like you and me

As I finished my song, the high school

drum-line samba band stepped in behind me. The group was decked out in their school shirts carrying their snare, bass, quads and cymbal instruments.

I looked down at the front row and smiled at Eddie. We'd been working together on our trap sound. Beside him sat my dad and Raymond. Then I walked back to take my place with the band. I put on my school shirt and joined the line. At the music teacher's signal, I started to drum.